SKELETON TREE

SKELETON TREE

Kim Ventrella

Illustrated by Victoria Assanelli

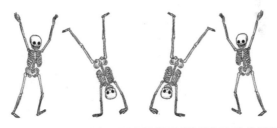

MACMILLAN CHILDREN'S BOOKS

First published in the US 2017 by Scholastic Press, an imprint of Scholastic Inc.

First published in the UK 2017 by Macmillan Children's Books
an imprint of Pan Macmillan
20 New Wharf Road, London N1 9RR
Associated companies throughout the world
www.panmacmillan.com

ISBN 978-1-5098-2867-8

1 3 5 7 9 8 6 4 2

A CIP catalogue record for this book is available from
the British Library.

Printed and bound by CPI Group (UK) Ltd, Croydon CR0 4YY

To my grandmother, who inspired me to write, and my grandfather, who taught me that whimsy and wonder often hide in the most ordinary places.

CHAPTER ONE

The day the rain stopped, Stanley Stanwright found a bone in the garden, poking up out of the dirt. It could have been a bean sprout, only it was white and hard and shaped like the tip of a little finger.

Stanley bent down to investigate. A shiver tickled his toes and curled all the way up the back of his neck. He touched the bone, quick, like it might bite. Cold seeped from the bone finger into his fleshy one. Wind slapped his face, blowing orange and brown leaves in from the neighbour's garden.

In that moment he felt like an explorer, like Dagger Rockbomb, hero of his favourite video game, *Skatepark Zombie Death Bash*. He might find something good hiding underground, like a dinosaur fossil. Or he might awaken a horde of slimy, flesh-eating zombies.

Some days were like that. One little thing happened, and nothing else was ever the same. The day Stanley's sister was born, for example. Or the night ten months ago, when his father took a taxi to the airport and never came back. Finding the finger bone felt the same way.

'Hey Bony-Butt, don't you know it's treasure time?' said Miren, racing down the cracked stone path and punching Stanley in the chest.

'Stop it! That hurt!' He stepped in front of the bone so Miren wouldn't see. The bone was his discovery. If Miren saw it, she would tell Mom and ruin everything. Mom never let him dig in the garden any more, since Dad left. 'You know what Mom said about running too fast.'

'I can breathe fine.' She shrugged and sprinted back to the house. 'Last one to treasure's a rotten nobody.'

'Egg,' said Stanley, shaking his head, but Miren was already gone.

Seven-year-olds get a lot of things wrong. Like how

Miren told him cows pee milk, and playing video games can make your fingers fall off. Stanley wondered if he'd said dumb things like that when he was seven.

He didn't think so.

When he was seven, he already knew how to read and change nappies and get Miren to take her medicine. The kind that smelt like canned worms. Even Mom and Dad didn't know how to do that.

'Stanley, you promised you'd be in the garage by five to ten. Your sister's waiting,' Mom said through the kitchen window. Her hair hung in wet curls around her chin. The one time something really important happened to him, and he had to leave. He felt bad about Miren going to the doctor, again, but why couldn't he do what he wanted just this once?

Before he went inside, Stanley snapped a shot of the bone with his old Polaroid camera. He would have used a phone, but he didn't have one, and Mom's was so old it couldn't do anything but make calls. The photo came out all grey and blobby, because Polaroids take ages to develop.

'Stanley, hurry up!' Mom shouted. He shoved the photo in his pocket and ran for the garage. Before he got in the car, he grabbed a Diet Coke from the mini-fridge he'd helped Dad pick out last year at a garage sale. The sides were still rusty, because Dad had left before he could repaint them.

In the car on the way to the doctor, Miren started coughing. Big, wet coughs that made her entire body shudder.

'I don't want to go to the doctor,' Miren said. She cupped her eyes and started to sniffle, like she was still three instead of seven.

Mom rolled down a window so some air could reach Stanley and Miren in the backseat. 'What about the treasure chest?' Stanley said.

Even though it was filled with baby stuff, Miren loved to pick out a toy from the inflatable treasure chest in Dr Cynthia's office. She loved it even more than cheeseburgers or those spinny things you get at the school carnival. She told him once. In those exact words.

She sucked in a deep breath that rattled in her chest. 'Nope, I changed my mind. I'm allowed to do that, you know?' Miren's jaw jutted out, tears teetering on the edge of her eyelids. 'I hate Dr Cynthia and her stupid treasures.'

Inside, Stanley sighed. A tiny part of his brain hated how Miren always acted like a baby, and how it was always up to him to make her feel better. But Stanley knew what to do when he felt like that.

He sliced off that part of his brain and fed it to his pet zombie. The zombie had green skin, two bulby eyes, and chomping teeth that were always hungry. His name was Slurpy, just like the pet zombie in *Skatepark Zombie Death Bash*.

'I want to go home!' Miren cried.

Chomp, chomp went the zombie in Stanley's head.

That was the nice thing about Slurpy. He was always ready to gobble up Stanley's problems. No matter how big and stupid.

'Why don't we play a game?' said Stanley. If Miren didn't stop screaming soon, he was pretty sure his head would actually explode.

'That's a good idea,' said Mom, hands clenching the steering wheel. She always got stressed out when she had to drive in traffic. 'Why don't you play I Spy? OK, sweetie?'

Miren squinched up her face, suspicious. 'What if I don't want to play?'

The stoplight turned red at the last minute, and Mom slammed on the brakes.

Stanley knew it was time to step in. 'Come on,

Mir-Bear. I'll even let you go first.'

'And second?'

'All right, and second.'

'OK.' She squeezed her eyes shut, which she always did when she was thinking really hard, and then she blurted out, 'I spy with my little eye something white hiding in the garden that Stanley doesn't want me to know about!' Miren was so excited, she pounded her fists on the seat, knocking over Stanley's drink.

'Ugh, stop doing that!' Stanley snatched his can and wiped up the bit that had spilt with the inside of his T-shirt. In his mind, he fed a little bit more of his frustration to Slurpy.

'Tell me, Bony-Butt! Bony-Butt, Bony-Butt! Tell me about your secret!'

'I don't have any secret!' Stanley didn't mean to shout, but he couldn't help it. Miren always got whatever she wanted, no matter what, but the bone was different. It was his. Besides, the last thing Stanley needed was for Mom to find out about the bone. She'd probably call pest control to come remove it. Since Dad left, she hated everything that reminded her of him, like dusty books or digging or the smell of his cinnamon aftershave.

In the front seat, Mom turned up the radio so loud it was mostly static.

Miren curled into a tiny ball and buried her head in her hands. Stanley didn't like seeing her like that, but sometimes she made him so angry. Good thing he had Slurpy to keep the whole brain-exploding situation under control.

'Let's just keep playing, OK?' he said.

Miren didn't answer. She curled up tighter and sniffled into her hair. That was her little sister superpower: No matter how annoying she got, she could always make you feel bad for yelling at her.

'I'll let you go first, second, and third,' he said, staring at the droplets of liquid sinking into the fabric.

Miren peeked out from behind her fingers. 'What about fourth?'

'Fine, you can go fourth, too.'

'I spy with my little eye . . .' Miren paused. Stanley was sure she was going to say something else about the bone, but just then the car lurched into the Spring Hill Pediatric Clinic.

Mom pulled Stanley aside once they got to the waiting room. 'Thank you for taking care of Miren back there . . . It's just . . . things have been really hard lately.'

She squeezed him so tight her orange peel shampoo clogged up his nostrils. 'I'm proud of you, Stanley. You've been a big help with your little sister. I hope you know that?'

For a moment, Stanley felt guilty for keeping a secret from Mom and Miren, but only for a moment. 'It's OK, Mom. No big deal.'

They sat down in comfy chairs with stiff arms. Mom flipped through a copy of *Dog Fancy* magazine. She ran her chipped fingernails over a picture of a Pekingese with perfect, flowy hair. Last year, she'd saved $1,500 to go to school to be a dog groomer, but then she'd spent it all on Miren's doctor bills.

'She'll get better soon,' Mom always said.

Stanley sure hoped so. If Mom could be a dog groomer instead of a cashier at Walgreens, things would be better, like before Dad left. She would smile more, and she could work from home, so Ms Francine wouldn't have to come watch them after school. And maybe Stanley could finally afford a computer that didn't crash every time he tried to install the latest version of *PixelBlock*. Or a camera that didn't take a hundred years to develop.

'The doctor's ready for you now,' said a nurse in light

purple scrubs. She gave Miren a lollipop shaped like a duck. The kind of thing you'd give a two-year-old. 'Follow me, sweetheart.'

'We'll be back in a few minutes,' Mom said. 'Find a magazine to read.'

Stanley never got to see the doctor with Miren and Mom. Like all of a sudden he was too young to hear about her problems. He slouched down in his chair and stared at the wall. It was covered in faded Halloween decorations. If he had an iPad, like Jaxon, he could play *PixelBlock* or *Ancient Aliens Attack!* or, even better, *Skatepark Zombie Death Bash*.

Instead, he picked up an old copy of *National Geographic* magazine. His dad used to buy him a subscription to it every year, but this last year he'd forgotten. Stanley skimmed past articles about owls and hunters in Alaska until he found a section about some guys in Africa who had uncovered the skeleton of a new type of dinosaur. One nobody had ever heard of before. An image flashed inside his head. There he was, wiping sweat from his brow as he swung his pickaxe into the rock. Ping, ping! The rock would crumble away, and there, underneath . . . a bone.

The daydream faded and was replaced by an image

of a finger sticking up through blades of grass. He still had the archaeology toolbox his dad had given him for Christmas two years ago. It had chisels and tiny brushes for uncovering bones. Going to Egypt or India or somewhere far away to dig for bones would be amazing, but what if he had an undiscovered species buried in his own garden?

He flipped through the rest of the magazine, and then his heart stopped. On the back cover was an ad for something called the Young Discoverer's Prize. It showed a picture of a boy holding a dinosaur tooth in his hand, but that wasn't the best part. Next to the boy's head, in puffy gold text, was the number ten followed by three zeros. As in $10,000.

Stanley skimmed all the way to the end of the ad, his palms tingling. 'Send us a picture of your discovery by midnight on October 31, and you and one guest will get a chance to win a trip to a real archaeological dig site worth $10,000!'

That was a lot of money, but it wasn't the part that leapt off the page and pinged, pinged, pinged in Stanley's head. The article said, 'you and one guest.' Stanley scanned the fine print. The guest could be anyone the winner wanted, as long as they were over eighteen. Well, that was fine by Stanley.

Dad might not be good at returning calls or checking his email, but if Stanley won this contest, he'd *have* to come and see him. He'd be his one guest. Archaeology had been Dad's one true dream, before he gave it up to go to law school. No way he would turn down a trip as awesome as this one, no matter how busy he was at work.

The door to the doctor's office swung open. Stanley had to think fast. He ripped the page out of the magazine and slipped it into his pocket before Mom could see. He knew that tearing up other people's magazines was wrong, and Mom would flip if she saw it, but he had no choice. The contest was too important.

'The specialist will call you to set up an appointment.' The nurse put a hand on Mom's shoulder. 'We'll find out what's going on. Don't you worry, Ms Stanwright.'

'Look, Stanley, I got a horsey and a sticky hand. See?'

The sticky hand slapped Stanley's forehead. 'Yup, I see.'

Miren giggled. 'Hold up your hand.'

'OK.' Stanley sighed.

Miren gave him a high five with the sticky hand.

'Amazing,' Stanley said.

'Let's go, you two. I've got to be at work by twelve.' Mom's eyes were red, like she'd been crying.

'What's wrong?' Stanley said as they walked out the front doors into a drizzly rain.

'Help your sister get strapped in, OK?'

Miren gave him a big, wet kiss on the forehead when they dropped her off at Happy Friends PlayHouse, aka baby day care. 'Bye Stanley, I'm sorry I called you Bony-Butt, so don't be mad at me, OK?'

Stanley couldn't help but laugh. Miren might be mega annoying, but she was still his little sister. Also, she had a sad face that made her look exactly like a baby spider monkey he'd once seen on the nature channel. It was her second little sister superpower, and it was impossible to ignore. 'OK, I guess I'm not mad at you. For now.'

'Score one for team me!' Miren punched the air and ran for the front doors, Mom chasing after her.

Stanley was too old for day care, and Ms Francine had that Saturday off, so he got to spend the day at Jaxon's house. Which was way better than sitting at home all day while Ms Francine boiled cabbage and played sad songs on the radio.

Outside, rain splattered the car window, making

Stanley's reflection go all long and wobbly. They pulled up to a stoplight, and Stanley caught Mom frowning at a doctor's bill in her lap. The edges of her mouth went all creasy, and he thought he knew why. Down at the bottom of the page was a number in bold, red type. He couldn't see the first part, but it ended in three zeros.

A car honked behind them. Mom stuffed the bill back into her bag and slammed on the accelerator.

'Have fun today,' she said once they got to Jaxon's house. 'Call me if you need me.'

Stanley didn't say anything. He was too busy thinking about the Young Discoverer's Prize. Maybe he could trade in the trip for cash. He was sure $10,000 would be enough to pay off Miren's doctor bills, maybe even with enough left over to buy a new camera or an iPad. But then, he might never get to see Dad.

'Sweetie, are you all right? You look a million miles away.'

'What? Oh, it's nothing, I'm fine.' He looked at Mom, the way her eyes were still pink and puffy. 'Did something bad happen today at the doctor's?'

Mom's thin lips cracked into a smile. 'Oh, Stanley, you don't need to worry about that. It's just . . .' The words caught in her throat. 'Promise me you'll have fun today, OK?'

'OK, Mom.'

Stanley watched the car drive away. He wished Mom would tell him what she was thinking instead of always keeping secrets. He crammed his hands into his pockets, and that was when he remembered the photo.

He smoothed it out and held up his jacket to keep it from getting wet. It didn't look like a grey blob any more. It was definitely a finger bone. And it wasn't pointing straight in the air, like it had been when he'd snapped the shot. It was pointing directly at him.

CHAPTER TWO

Stanley helped Jaxon count the fence slats in the garden to make sure they were still there. One hundred and fifty-two, just like last week.

'Sorry,' Jaxon said once they'd finished. He flattened down his cloud of black hair and stared at his feet. 'You really don't have to help me.'

'No big deal,' Stanley said. 'Let's go inside and play *Skatepark Zombie Death Bash*.'

Jaxon only paused at the door once to look back at the fence. Stanley could hear him counting under his breath. He tapped the side of his head, like he was trying to get water out of his ears, and then he went inside. Jaxon had something called OCD. Stanley didn't remember what it stood for, but it mostly meant that Jaxon worried about things more than other people. Like how many slats were in the fence, or how many times he touched the light switch before he went to the skatepark.

The one in real life, not the one full of hungry zombies.

'Mother of god, he just ate that baby's face off,' Jaxon said.

Stanley watched the zombie dislocate his jaw and eat the baby's face in a single bite. 'Epic.'

'Now he's nibbling on the toes.' Jaxon laughed so hard he cried. A zombie snuck up behind him and started to gnaw on his shoulder.

'Hey, look out!'

They battled the baby-eating zombies, and then another horde all dressed like nuns in black robes and pointy hats.

'My fingers hurt,' Jaxon said after playing for four hours straight. 'Want a snack? My mom made thumbprint cookies, and we have a giant block of cheese. Like, as big as my head.'

'Sure,' Stanley said, but he didn't get up. He'd been waiting to tell Jaxon about the bone ever since he got there, but it had to be the right time. This was big. Bigger than big. And if there was anyone who could help him win the contest, and be trusted with the biggest secret of all time, it was Jaxon.

And OK, maybe Stanley hoped Jaxon might be

jealous of his discovery, just a little. The way he'd felt when Jaxon brought back that lava rock from Hawaii or that genuine shark tooth from his trip to Florida.

'Hey, what are you hiding?' said Jaxon.

'I've got a secret, I guess. You wouldn't be interested. Anyway, let's get a snack.'

'Whoa. Hold up. Why wouldn't I want to know your secret?'

'Because you hate everything that is awesome,' Stanley said. 'And you only love boring things like giant blocks of cheese.'

'You have to tell me your secret,' Jaxon said, turning on Stanley. 'Remember last week, how I saved you from that horde of zombie cheerleaders?'

'True.' Stanley rubbed his chin. 'OK, I guess I could tell you. On one condition.'

'What?' Jaxon sank to the floor, groaning. 'You are twenty-five kinds of impossible.'

'Why twenty-five?'

'Just tell me!'

'Promise you won't blab?' Not that Jaxon would. He was an expert at keeping secrets, even about that time Stanley accidentally put a worm in Miren's chicken noodle soup.

'Gah, I promise already! Spill it!'

'OK.' Stanley told Jaxon about the bone growing in his garden, and how he was going to win the contest and bring his dad on the best trip ever. Only he didn't actually say that last part. Jaxon always got really quiet whenever Stanley brought up his dad, like he was afraid he'd say something that would hurt Stanley's feelings.

'You realize bones don't grow in gardens, right?'

'Time for snacks, Bunny-Bean. Cheese and crackers and sweet tea,' Jaxon's mom trilled from the kitchen.

'But you know what does end up in gardens?' Jaxon said. 'Dead bodies.'

'Dead dinosaur bodies,' Stanley corrected.

Jaxon shook his head. 'No, for real. This is just like the Darby Brothers' Mystery #148, *The Case of the Missing Cat*.'

'This has nothing to do with cats,' Stanley said. 'Gah, why do you have to ruin my dreams?'

'Bunny-Bean, tell Stanley we've got cookies. Snickerdoodle or chocolate chip.'

'Ugh, we'll be there in a minute!' Jaxon said. 'Yes, it does. In #148, James Darby finds a bone in his backyard. He thinks it's a dead body or something, but it ends up being his mom's cat.'

'She murdered her own cat?'

'No, it died when she was a kid and she buried it.' Jaxon stood up and brushed the wrinkles from his *PixelBlock* T-shirt. 'Not everything's a big mystery, you know?' Jaxon fixed Stanley with his grown-up stare.

'Whatever, I guess I'll dig it up myself.' Stanley stomped out of the room, like he was really angry. 'Oh, and I guess you won't want to see this.' He waved the photo inside the doorway and then sprinted down the hall.

Jaxon tackled him just feet from the garden, his elbow digging into Stanley's rib cage. 'Show me!'

'OK, OK, geez.'

Jaxon's forehead scrunched up like a raisin. 'That . . .' His breath got all scratchy in his throat. '. . . is a finger bone.'

'Right! And see how it's pointing? The weird part is—'

'Pointing?' Jaxon said, turning the photo so Stanley could see it.

'It's more like a big question mark. Look how it's all curvy on the end . . . Stanley?'

Stanley didn't answer. The inside of his mouth had gone dry, like he'd eaten a hundred blocks of salty cheese without a single drop of water. The first time the picture had moved, he thought he'd just imagined it, but now, if Jaxon could see it, too . . .

'Hey, what's wrong?' Jaxon knocked on Stanley's forehead. 'Did a zombie eat your brain or something?'

'Yeah,' Stanley managed. 'Or something.'

CHAPTER THREE

Stanley's mom picked him up at eight, and they got McDonald's milkshakes and French fries for dinner. Then she drove them out to the lake so they could eat their food in the car, looking up at the stars. You could see a lot more stars by the lake than in the city, but not half as many as when he and Dad went digging for fossils at Merrell State Park. Out there, the sky looked like a velvet blanket sprinkled with gold and white and blue-green glass.

'That one's called Priscilla.'

Miren pointed at a glowing orange star. 'Or maybe Tiffany.'

'Tiffany?' Stanley said, choking on a French fry. 'That's Mars. You know, the planet? That's why it's bigger than all the other ones. Don't they teach you anything in second grade?'

Miren shook her head. 'Nope, it's definitely Tiffany.'

Stanley stuffed a French fry in his mouth to keep from laughing. Miren said so many funny things that if he laughed at all of them, he'd never finish eating. Also, she'd probably get mad and tell Mom he was making fun of her.

'Did you have a good time at day care today?' Stanley said. He scooped a glob of milkshake on to the end of his fry and gobbled down the salty-sweet mixture.

Miren shrugged. 'It's not day care, that's for babies. It's PlayHouse. And not really. Samson pooed his pants . . . again. And it got on the slide, and so Mrs Schwartz made everyone go inside and do dumb dot paintings after that.'

'Yuck, poo slide.' Stanley could still remember when one of the kids at his day care had done something like that, only in the water fountain.

Stanley was glad he wasn't a little kid any more.

He looked up at the stars while his mom sat in the front seat, reading her dog grooming textbook with a torch.

'How was work?' Stanley said.

She didn't answer. Stanley peeked around the seat and saw white earbuds dangling from her ears. He thought about tapping her shoulder, but he knew how much being a dog groomer meant to her. And she almost never got time to study.

'She can't hear you,' Miren said, holding her milkshake in front of her face like a shield. 'You can tell me your secret now.'

'What?' Stanley nearly choked on another fry.

'About the thing you found in the garden.'

'I don't know what you're talking about.' He checked to make sure Mom's face was still buried in her book.

Miren coughed so hard it sounded like she'd swallowed a rusty engine. 'I promise I won't tell.' She slid down in the seat until her cheek smooshed against the seat belt. 'It'll be our secret, pleeeeease.'

As she said it, she coughed again, and her body shook so much the lid popped off her milkshake and a white blob oozed down the front of her shirt. She froze, her cheeks burned red, and then her forehead crumpled.

Three sure signs she was about to burst into tears if he didn't do something fast.

He wanted the bone to be something for him and Dad alone, but he knew he'd have to tell Miren sooner or later. Probably sooner. That was her little sister superpower at work again.

Her bottom lip quivered. That meant the volcano was about to explode. Tears and screaming and Mom would have to give up studying and drive home in three . . . two . . .

'Fine.' Stanley slumped down in the seat beside Miren, defeated. He got a napkin and wiped the milkshake from her T-shirt. 'But you have to promise on Baby Ashleigh and Stripy Pony and all of your toys that you won't tell Mom . . . not ever. Promise?'

Miren stuck out a milkshake-covered pinky. 'I swear.'

'You don't need to swear, just promise.'

'OK, I promise.'

So Stanley told Miren about archaeologists and old bones and how maybe the thing in the garden was an undiscovered dinosaur. He didn't tell her about the Young Discoverer's Prize, or how he planned to take Dad along on the expedition. If he did, Miren would want to come, too, and then Dad would spend the whole time entertaining her instead of hanging out with him. Just like when they were little kids.

'I wanna help with the digging,' Miren said. 'Mrs Nelson at PlayHouse said I'm a really good helper, because the first time someone pooed on the slide, I ran and got the wet wipes and—'

'You can be my assistant,' Stanley said, deciding he'd heard enough poo-slide stories for one night. 'But you have to do exactly what I say and promise not to mess anything up.'

'I already said I promise.'

'That was about the secret. This is about the bone. There's a special way you have to dig up old bones.'

'I know, Stanley, I don't have mashed potatoes for brains.'

'OK, if you say so. Can you find that gardening set Uncle Morris gave you for your birthday? We might be able to use it.'

'Yeah, I keep it under my bed next to Stripy Pony and Baby Ashleigh and—'

'Perfect. Meet me in the garden after breakfast and bring the gardening set with you.' Inside, he cringed at the idea of digging with Miren around, but at least that way he'd be able to keep an eye on her.

'OK,' Miren said. 'Stanley?'

'Yeah?'

'What if it's not a dinosaur, but an alien or a dead vampire or something scary?'

'Vampires can't die, dummy.'

'I know, but what if it's an alien? With laser eyes, like in that stupid video game you're always playing?'

Stanley squeezed Miren's shoulder. 'Don't worry. It's not an alien, and if it is it'll be a nice one.'

'Promise?'

'Definitely.' Stanley smoothed down Miren's wispy brown hair. 'Hey, why didn't you eat any of your food?'

'Not hungry,' Miren said. She closed her eyes and coughed into what was left of her milkshake.

'You feel OK?'

Miren shook her head. Stanley hugged her to his chest, and they watched the stars wink at them through the dirty car window.

CHAPTER FOUR

Stanley woke to the smell of boiling cabbage.

'Good morning, little Stanley. Momma had to go to work early, too bad for her, just look at all this rain.' Ms Francine swatted a wrinkled hand towards the dining room window. She wore a sweater that looked like a woolly mammoth hide, with a fuzzy purple scarf wrapped around her head. 'I'm making borscht for dinner. Good for the digestion.'

Great. 'What about for breakfast?' Stanley said, watching rain splash the windows. When Dad had lived at home, they always had eggs and bacon in the morning, or at least cereal.

'Cinnamon toast with raisins. You like this.'

Stanley sat at the dining room table, picking the raisins out of his cinnamon toast. Dad would have never fixed something like that for breakfast; he knew how much Stanley hated raisins.

Ms Francine clucked her tongue. 'How will you grow big and strong if you never eat? In Kyrgyzstan, we ate tea for breakfast and lunch, and maybe we got borscht for dinner. If we were lucky.'

'You can't eat tea,' Stanley said. He took a bite of toast. Despite the gooey raisins, it tasted sweet and crunchy and delicious.

'If you're hungry, you can eat what you want,' said Ms Francine.

Stanley ate more toast, and Ms Francine stirred the cabbage and told him about life in Kyrgyzstan. He only half listened. How was he going to dig up a dinosaur skeleton in all this rain?

'We walked seven miles each way, with snow up to our waists,' Ms Francine was saying. 'Never would we frown over this little bit of rain.' She waved a wooden spoon at him. 'Why so sad today? You won't melt.'

'I don't know . . . nothing,' Stanley said. No way he was going to tell Ms Francine about the bone.

'I see. This nothing wouldn't happen to be in the back garden, would it?' Ms Francine flashed a crooked smile. 'Don't be so surprised. I see you looking out there. You know,' she said, 'there is such a thing as a raincoat.'

'You mean I can go outside?' Stanley said, suspicious.

'Go, play. If you wash away, I'll tell Momma it was my fault. Go, wake your sister. Tell her to eat breakfast first. And make sure she wears a scarf!'

Stanley had already tossed his plate in the sink and rushed off down the hall.

'Miren, get up. We have to go outside. Ms Francine is here, but she said it's OK.' He lowered his voice. 'And I don't think she's seen the you-know-what yet, at least not up close, so come on before she—'

Stanley stopped. He checked under the sheets and inside the wardrobe. No use. Miren wasn't there.

'Where's this sister of yours?' Ms Francine said when Stanley came back into the kitchen.

'She's not in her bed.'

'Invisible? Ah, I had this happen once.' Ms Francine ran a finger over her bristly chin. 'With my goat. We looked for him in the pasture and on the mountain. Nowhere. Then, one day, I walk by the shop, and there is Bakyt, my goat, munching all the clothes in the shop window. He had his own secret,' Ms Francine said, winking and tapping the side of her nose.

'This is important,' Stanley said. 'Miren's lost, and she's not a goat. She could run into the street and get squashed like Jaxon's cousin's brother's ferret.'

'Come,' said Ms Francine. 'Let's go look at your secret, and maybe Miren won't be so invisible any more.'

Stanley ran outside without his coat. Plump raindrops pelted his face. He wasn't even worried that Ms Francine would see the bone; he just wanted to find Miren.

'Miren!' he called through a wave of rain. Mud sucked at his socks as he ran, and then he saw her. She was crouched in the grass, staring at something white and knobby curving up out of the earth. It wasn't just the tip of a finger any more.

'What are you doing? You're going to freeze to death!' he shouted, even as relief warmed his soggy toes.

'It grew.' Her voice was quiet as an icy wind. 'And it's not a dino.'

Stanley leaned closer. Sure enough, the finger was at least an inch longer than it had been the day before, and Miren was right. It didn't look like a dinosaur bone any more.

Ms Francine put her hairy sweater around Miren and Stanley. It smelt like dust and cabbage, but it soaked up all the rain.

'They do that,' she said. 'Grow, I mean.'

Stanley turned to look at Ms Francine. Rain trickled down her wrinkled face and pooled in the hollows of her shoulders.

She shrugged. 'We have a tree like this in Kyrgyzstan. It happens.'

'It's not a tree,' Stanley said, but it had grown. Four white knuckles peeked through the mud, along with the tip of a thumb. He stared at it, hypnotized by that bone hand, not noticing the rain beating against his cheek. He could have stayed out there all day, looking at it, but then he felt Miren shiver against his skin.

'Maybe we should go inside, just for a little bit,' he said. He didn't want to leave the bone, but he also didn't want to end up with an ice cube for a little sister.

'Good idea,' Ms Francine said. 'We eat hot tea and cookies.'

'Come on, Mir-Bear. We'll dig later. Time to warm up.'

'OK,' Miren said through chattering teeth.

They went inside. Stanley only stopped once to look back at the bones. Maybe it was his imagination, but he could have sworn the finger twitched. Like it wanted him to come closer.

'Hurry up, my little fish. What will I say to Momma if you drown in your own garden?'

CHAPTER FIVE

Ms Francine made tea and baked cookies from a
tube. Stanley's favourite. Miren and Stanley changed
into dry clothes, and Ms Francine made a walkway with
newspapers so she wouldn't drip on the carpet.

'You're not going to tell anyone about the bone, are
you?' said Stanley, already dreading the answer.

'Who is this anyone?' said Ms Francine. 'Why
shouldn't they know about your discovery?'

'Please,' Stanley said. 'I promise to do the
dishes for a week.'

Ms Francine wiggled her eyebrows but didn't
say anything.

'Fine, *two* weeks.'

'Deal, but remember, little Stanley, some secrets don't like to be kept. They grow feet and tiptoe away in the night.'

'That's not how secrets work.'

'If you say so.' Ms Francine picked up cookie crumbs on the tip of her thumb and flicked them into the bin. 'Maybe, after tea, we can go to the museum,' she said. 'Then you can look at bones without getting all wet.'

'No thanks,' said Stanley. He didn't care about bones someone else had already dug up. He wanted to discover something new. Something he could use to win the Young Discoverer's Prize.

'I see,' Ms Francine said. 'Then you two can help me make borscht until the rain stops.'

Miren coughed into her napkin. It sounded like her lungs were filled with a giant, sticky slimeball.

'I don't like borscht,' Miren said.

'I know, little one. But borscht likes you.'

⊷━⊶

The rain didn't stop that night, or the next morning. If anything, it got worse. Water slid under the garage and pooled behind the boxes of Christmas ornaments. If Dad were there, he would know how to fix the leak, but Mom just ignored it.

'Make sure Miren brushes her teeth,' Mom said, buzzing the hair dryer over her dripping curls.

'She can do it herself,' Stanley said, but not loud enough for anyone to hear.

'I don't want to you can't make me!' Miren blurted out the words all at once and then clamped her jaw shut.

Stanley squirted toothpaste on to her brush. Inside, Slurpy the zombie reared his ugly head. Stanley wasn't even supposed to be inside, playing babysitter; he was supposed to be outside, digging. 'Here, I'm not gonna brush them for you. Just do what Mom says.'

'No way!' She shook her head. 'I wanna go see the bone. You said I could be your assistant, remember?'

'Shhh,' Stanley said. 'Don't let Mom hear.' It was bad enough that Ms Francine knew about his secret. He didn't need Mom to find out, too. 'Besides, we both have to go to school, whether you like it or not.'

'I'm not going to school until I see the bone.' Miren drew in a deep sigh, like she was swallowing the problems of the whole world.

'Can you please just brush your teeth?'

'Leave me alone!' Miren dropped the toothbrush and glittery pink toothpaste splattered all over Stanley's new shoes, the ones he'd bought with the last of his lawn-mowing money.

Stanley balled up his hands and something inside his head ignited. He wished Miren would do what he said just once, instead of whining and wasting his time and making life harder than it had to be. Why couldn't she just listen?

He took a deep breath. If he wasn't careful, his anger would unleash a fire so hot he would burn to a crisp, like that time Ms Francine tried to grill. But then Miren started to laugh. She laughed and laughed, and the sound grated on Stanley's nerves. In his head, Slurpy munched up all of his bad thoughts, but he must not have munched fast enough, because something terrible happened.

Stanley screamed. He didn't say anything; he just screamed, so loud the back of his throat started to itch.

'What did you do to her?' Mom swooped around the corner, eyes wide. Miren, of course, had started crying. Stanley tried to answer, but his throat was sore from all the screaming. Also, he didn't know what to say. He'd never screamed like that before in his whole life. For once, he was glad Dad wasn't there to see him scream like that.

'Go clean up your shoes, Stanley,' said Mom. The side of her mouth pinched like she was trying hard not to scream herself. 'We'll talk about this when I get home . . . I'm really disappointed in you.'

Stanley didn't talk to anyone all morning once he got to school, not even when Mr Erickson asked him to help with Halloween decorations for the class party. At lunch, he sat at a corner table by himself. Screaming had got out most of his anger, but some of it was still there, bubbling beneath the surface like one of Ms Francine's stinky pots of borscht.

'What are you doing way over here?' said Jaxon, plopping his tray down next to Stanley. 'Yuck, there's a bug in my macaroni.'

Stanley peeked out from under his tangly hair. 'That's just a speck.'

Jaxon picked out the speck with his fork. 'I can't eat this now.' He wiped the speck on a napkin, folded up the napkin into a tiny ball, and walked it to the bin.

'Just eat it.' Stanley could tell he sounded really angry about the speck for no reason, but he couldn't help it. Jaxon could make a problem out of anything. Like that time they were late to art class because Jaxon was convinced he'd left his locker open, even though he'd already checked it five times. Stanley bet Jaxon had never had a real problem in his entire life.

Jaxon pushed the tray towards Stanley. A tiny shudder ran through his body, like the thought of eating macaroni with a speck in it was the worst thing in the world. 'No way. You take it. I'm not hungry any more.'

'You are so . . .' Something hard caught in Stanley's throat. He tried to swallow it, but it kept coming back up.

'What?' Jaxon said, sounding hurt.

'Nothing.'

'Just say it. I'm so what?'

Inside his head, Slurpy pummelled a slimeball to smithereens, and the gooey green bits splattered all over Stanley's brain. At least that was what it felt like. He was sick of always biting his tongue. He was angry, and for once he wanted to say exactly what he thought.

'Crazy! Happy? You're so crazy! It was just a stupid speck.'

Jaxon left his tray and went to sit with Zander and Ian. All the anger drained out of Stanley, and he couldn't believe he'd said that horrible thing. Jaxon was different, but he couldn't help it. And he was also Stanley's best friend. So what if he worried too much about macaroni specks?

He should go over and apologize, but he had no idea what to say. Plus, Zander and Ian would probably laugh at him and call him a loser, and then he'd never be able to show his face in the cafeteria again.

Instead, he stared out the window, all the time imagining how the day might have gone if Dad had been back. He could have brushed Miren's teeth, so Stanley's shoes wouldn't be ruined. Dad could have driven him to school and maybe even taken him out to McDonald's for lunch. Cheeseburgers and ice cream sundaes, Stanley's favourite.

Too bad Dad was fifteen hundred miles away in California.

By the time fourth period rolled around, Stanley had stubbed his toe on a locker door, got two warnings in

English class, and slipped in a puddle of water outside the boys' toilets.

OK, it wasn't water.

Slurpy did his best to guzzle down all of his problems, but he could only eat so much. Things were starting to get out of hand.

Jaxon and Stanley had fourth period social studies together. Stanley tried to sit in the back by the pencil sharpener, because he still didn't know how to make things better with Jaxon, but Ms. Waite made him go to his assigned seat.

'Hey,' Jaxon said, looking kind of sheepish.

'Hey,' Stanley said. 'Um . . .'

'Sorry about lunch,' said Jaxon, before Stanley could get any more words out. 'I know I act kind of crazy sometimes.' Jaxon fiddled with his Darby Brothers' wristwatch. 'Thanks for being my friend, Stanley.'

The worst thing was, Stanley could tell Jaxon really meant it. And he didn't even care if Zac or Cooper or whiny Melissa heard him. Stanley was the one who should be apologizing.

'Oh . . . um, OK.' Sometimes it felt like someone had snipped the cord that connected Stanley's brain to his mouth. Maybe Slurpy had got carried away with all his crunching. 'So . . . do you wanna come over after school?'

'Mr Stanwright, do you have something you'd like to share with the class?' said Ms Waite.

Stanley zipped his lips, but a few minutes later he slid something from his back pocket and passed it to Jaxon. It was the ad for the Young Discoverer's Prize. At the bottom, written in green gel pen, were the words, 'You don't need to say thank you.'

On the bus ride home, Stanley told Jaxon more about the Young Discoverer's Prize, and Jaxon, eager to help, told Stanley about the Darby Brothers' top ten rules for solving mysteries. Even though it was really boring, Stanley never once interrupted.

When he finished, Stanley blurted out the thing he'd been waiting to say to Jaxon all day. 'It grew,' Stanley said. 'You can see its knuckles now, and a thumb. It's definitely not a dinosaur. And yesterday, when it was raining . . .' Stanley took a deep breath. '. . . it moved.' Once the words were out of his mouth, Stanley was surprised to find his hands were shaking.

Jaxon let his copy of the *Darby Brothers' Official Mystery Handbook* fall open in his lap.

'What do you mean it moved?'

'It twitched. Like, I don't know, it didn't want me to go inside or something.' As he said it, invisible fireworks crackled on the back of his tongue. Like talking about the bone out loud made it more real or something.

'OK, now who's the one acting crazy?' Jaxon said. Stanley deserved that. 'You're forgetting about rule number seven: Never let your imagination get the better of you.'

'It wasn't my imagination,' Stanley said.

'Bones don't grow, not when they're already in the ground. That's a fact.' Jaxon loved facts, even more than he loved video games or the Darby Brothers' mysteries. It was one of the qualities that made him a good detective.

'It might be weird, but it's still a fact,' Stanley said. 'You'll see.'

•═══•

The bus dropped them off at the end of the street next to the rusty fire hydrant.

'This is called a hoe,' Ms Francine was saying to Miren when they came into the kitchen. 'And this is a spade.' She set it next to Miren's other garden tools on the table. 'I used one of these in Kyrgyzstan, to dig up potatoes from the side of the mountain. But we had to watch out for goats. They would come along and gobble up all of our hard work.'

Miren laughed. The sound grated in Stanley's ears. He looked down at his brand-new trainers. They used to be red, but now they were splattered all over with dried glitter toothpaste.

'Come on, Jaxon, let's go outside.' He tried to slip out the back door, but Miren was too fast.

'Hey!' She spun around in her chair. 'Where do you think you're going, Bony-Butt? I've got all my tools, and you promised I could dig, remember, so wait up!'

Stanley banged his forehead lightly on the screen door. Maybe, if he closed his eyes and wished hard enough, Miren would disappear.

'What is *that* doing here?' Miren scowled up at Jaxon, hands on her hips.

'*That* is my friend,' said Stanley. 'And don't pretend like you don't know his name. He's only been here like a thousand times.'

'I'm your assistant, you said so, not Jaxon with an *x*, which is a dumb way to spell a name, by the way. You'd better let me come dig with you, or else.'

'Or else what?' Stanley said, hot liquid bubbling up his throat. 'Or you'll ruin another pair of my shoes?'

'Play nice, my little goats.' Ms Francine clicked her tongue at them. 'Why so upset? The sun is out, the breeze is cool . . . and . . .' She pressed a finger to her temple. '. . . ah yes, if I'm not mistaken, this secret of yours, it's still growing.'

Miren punched the air and ran off towards Mom's room. 'I've gotta get something, don't leave without me. I'm warning you, Stanley!'

Jaxon shook his head. 'Darby Brothers' rule number six: Always think before you act.'

'Who are these Darby Brothers? Friends of yours?' said Ms Francine.

Stanley left Jaxon to explain while he went to his room to get his tools. A lump filled his throat as he opened the rusty metal box. It still smelt like his dad. Dusty books and motor oil and cinnamon chewing gum. He found a ratty pack in the top drawer and took out a stick. The gum was so old it snapped when he tried to bend it.

He shoved the pack to the bottom of the box. He took out a pick and a trowel and closed the lid. Maybe he didn't need the whole box after all. Besides, if Mom came home and saw it out in the garden, she'd get a sad look on her face, and he didn't need to see that. He stuck some paintbrushes from Uncle Morris's paint set in his pocket and ran back to the kitchen.

'Come on, grab that gardening stuff,' he told Jaxon. 'Where's Miren anyway? She better not be outside already. I don't want her messing everything up.'

Ms Francine didn't answer. She was too busy frowning at Jaxon. 'How do these little boys know so much about solving mysteries anyway?'

'They're not little boys.' Jaxon threw up his hands. 'The Darby Brothers are twelve, like us.'

'Ah,' said Ms Francine, 'then they are old men.'

'"All you need to be a good detective is curiosity and attention to detail,"' Jaxon quoted. 'Come on, Stanley, let's go.'

The boys gathered up the gardening stuff and let the back door slam behind them. The broken gutter shuddered with the sudden impact, belching a wad of mouldy leaves on to the cracked birdbath. Miren was not in the garden. Where could she be?

'Some people ask too many questions,' Jaxon said when they were sure Ms Francine couldn't hear.

Stanley bit back a smile. He stopped dead when he saw the bone.

Five knobby fingers reached up towards the sky. Like someone buried alive trying to claw free. Only this someone hadn't been alive for a very long time.

CHAPTER SIX

'Bones don't grow,' Jaxon said for the third time, chewing his nails. 'They just don't.'

Stanley took out one of his paintbrushes and dusted dirt from the fingers. It reminded him of the trip to Merrell State Park, when he and Dad had discovered a real dinosaur tooth together.

'This is going to be perfect for the Young Discoverer's Prize,' Stanley said.

'Oh yeah, I still have your paper, by the way.' Jaxon handed Stanley the ad for the contest. Stanley couldn't help but notice his hand was shaking.

'Hey, what's up? You look like you're going to throw up.'

'There has to be an explanation,' Jaxon said. 'Maybe it's tree roots. You know, pushing up from underneath, making it look like the bones are growing.'

'There aren't any trees.' Just the crumbly shed and a few shrubs that reminded Stanley of globby hairballs, like the kind Mrs Anderson's cat was always coughing up on the front lawn.

'It could be groundwater? Or microearthquakes. The ground shifts all the time, you know?' Jaxon leaned an inch closer. 'It's not moving, by the way.'

'Just wait.' A shivery finger traced a circle around Stanley's brain, kind of like before, when the bone first grew. He couldn't explain it, but he knew it would happen again. Even if it seemed impossible. Even if, maybe, he didn't want it to.

They waited . . . and waited. Once, it looked like the hand moved, but even Stanley had to admit it was probably the wind.

'Let's just start digging,' said Stanley. 'The important thing is to get the bones out where we can see them.'

He jabbed the trowel into the ground a few feet away from the hand. He didn't want to risk cracking any of the bones. The spade clanked and bounced back, like he had hit metal instead of soft mud.

'That's not normal,' Jaxon said. He tugged on his ear, like he'd just gone swimming and it was clogged with water. 'Here, let me try.'

Jaxon dragged Miren's tiny rake across the dirt, not looking at all happy to be that close to the bones. The metal spokes skipped over the surface like nails scratching a chalkboard. Jaxon dropped the rake and started counting the fingers on his right hand over and over under his breath. 'This is so, seriously, not normal.'

'Relax,' Stanley said. 'I've got an idea.' He raised the pick over his head and aimed at a spot a foot or so away from the bones.

He was about to strike when Miren rushed outside, carrying something in her hands. Her Stripy Pony flip-flops slapped the paving stones as she ran.

'Stanley, wait! I'm going to take a picture –' The flip-flops got all tangled up on her feet, and the next thing Stanley knew, she splatted face-first on the ground. Stanley's Polaroid camera flew from her hands and hit Mom's frog statue with a sickening crunch.

'No!' Stanley ran to pick up the camera, and it fell into three separate pieces in his hands. 'Miren, why do you have to ruin everything?'

The words tumbled out of his mouth before he could

stop them. In his head, Slurpy ballooned to the size of a planet. All of Stanley's pent-up rage whirled around inside him, sizzling, sulphuric gases, billowing up and out, until finally . . . Slurpy exploded, sending pink brain goop everywhere.

Miren wailed and pawed at her bloody knees. Stanley squeezed his eyes shut. He just wanted her to be quiet; was that too much to ask? But now, with Slurpy gone, all of the anger he'd been eating up seeped into Stanley's body. It slithered into his veins and sent heat waves radiating down his spine. He had to let it out somehow, so he said what he was really thinking: 'Miren, sometimes I wish you didn't even exist.'

Miren stopped crying. She glared up at him and, almost too quiet to hear, said, 'I hate you.'

The words settled like cold stones in the bottom of Stanley's stomach. Ms Francine ran outside, scooped Miren into her arms, and took her into the kitchen, but Stanley hardly noticed. She didn't yell at him, but a few minutes later she brought out a tray with two glasses of peppery lemonade and asked a question that made him feel even worse than what Miren had said. 'You do what you want, little Stanley. Ms Francine is not your mother. But let me ask you this. What is worse? A broken camera, or a broken little sister?'

Stanley wanted to say a broken camera, but he got the point. The weird lemonade left a slimy coating inside his throat. His brain still felt like it was made of gloppy zombie guts, and he kind of wanted to throw up.

'Maybe you should go say you're sorry,' Jaxon said. He backed away from Stanley when he said it, like he was scared of him.

Stanley sighed so hard he thought his lungs might collapse. He didn't answer for a long time, but deep down he knew Jaxon was right. Even if Miren was super annoying and had probably screwed up his chances of winning the Young Discoverer's Prize. How could he take the winning picture without a camera?

'I'll be back in a minute,' he said.

On his way to her room, he passed the picture of him pushing Miren in her stroller outside the tiger enclosure at the zoo. Little did he know back then that having a sister would be kind of like adopting a baby tiger. They both started out cute and cuddly, until they grew teeth and claws and began destroying everything.

Stanley found Miren scrunched up under her Stripy Pony covers. He looked around to make sure Ms Francine wasn't listening. It was one thing to apologize; it was another thing to admit to Ms Francine that he was wrong.

'I'm sorry I got mad, OK?' The words stuck in his throat, but he was glad once he'd got them out.

Miren twitched under the blankets but didn't answer. 'I mean, you did break my camera . . .' Stanley waited, and waited. When Miren didn't say anything, he groaned. 'Fine, I just thought I'd say I'm sorry. If you don't wanna come out and dig with us, that's up to you.'

'You mean I can be your assistant again?' Miren shot out of the covers. 'Your real, official assistant?'

'I guess.' Stanley was already starting to regret his decision to apologize.

'Yes!' Miren slid out of bed and then stopped. 'Stanley?'

'What?'

'Do you really wish I didn't exist?'

Stanley looked at Miren, with her scraggly hair and too-thin arms. He remembered back when she was three how she always wanted to arm wrestle, and how he always let her win no matter what. Even when she called him stupid names like Bony-Butt. And he remembered that day at the zoo, when she cried because one of the elephants had a hurt leg, and how he was the only one who could make her feel better. 'No, I didn't mean it.'

'OK.' Miren hopped down and spanked Stanley's butt. 'Then I guess I don't hate you, either. Last one outside's a rotten nobody!'

Egg, Stanley thought but didn't say. Miren raced outside, her breath coming out all wheezy. 'Give me that!'

She snatched the pick from Jaxon's hands and swung it into the dirt. Stanley cringed, sure she was going to ruin his discovery.

Clang! The pick shot back, almost hitting Miren in the face.

'Hey!' said Miren. 'It's like he doesn't want anyone to dig him up.'

'*He?*' said Stanley.

'This doesn't make any sense,' Jaxon said, screwing up his forehead. 'There has to be a reasonable explanation. I know! Let's try to dig somewhere else. That way, we'll know if it's just this spot where we can't dig, or the whole garden.'

Stanley, Jaxon, and Miren used their tools to make holes all over the garden. The metal parts slid easily into the wet dirt. Digging with Miren ended up not being so bad, since it kept her occupied and Stanley mostly didn't have to listen to her blab.

'It's just this one spot,' Stanley said, shaking his head.

'What kind of bones don't let you dig them up?'

'Highly illogical ones.' Jaxon came over to stand beside Stanley. 'This would never happen in a Darby Brothers' mystery.'

They stared down at the hand. As they did, the little finger shot back.

Jaxon screamed.

Stanley yelped.

Miren stood still, mouth forming a tiny O.

Nobody moved for a full minute, and then Stanley crept over to the hand, goose pimples arching up his spine. He touched the tip of the knobby little finger. The bone was cold and hard beneath his skin.

'What are you doing?' Jaxon whispered. 'Didn't you see it move?'

'I bet nobody else in the whole world is going to discover something like this,' Stanley said.

Images raced through Stanley's mind. He could see the headline now: 'World's Youngest Archaeologist Discovers Moving Skeleton.' He would be famous. Even without his camera, he'd find a way. His mom wouldn't have to work at Walgreens any more. They'd live in a mansion, and he'd have a hundred iPads, and his dad would be so happy he would –

'Momma! You're home!' Miren ran towards the house, and Mom picked her up and spun her around.

'What's your mom doing home so early?' Jaxon said.

'I don't know. Help me hide it. She can't find out.'

'Why?'

'Just do it.'

Stanley and Jaxon scooted in front of the hand, blocking it from view. If she found out now, everything would be ruined. She'd call the police or the Department of Health or something, and guys in white suits would come take the bones away.

'You're home early,' he said, reaching for Miren, pulling her towards him before she could open her big mouth and –

'Momma, look what we found!' Miren pointed behind Stanley's shins, smiling her stupid spider monkey smile. She jumped up and down, and then her smile collapsed when she looked at Stanley's face.

'What are you two hiding?' said Mom.

She peeked behind Stanley's legs, then stared down at the tools and out at the garden.

'Stanley Stanwright.' She smoothed down her frizzy curls. This was it, the instant she put an end to his dreams of winning the contest. 'Can you explain to me how all of these holes got here?' Suddenly, her voice sounded brittle, like it might crack.

'You see, Mrs Stanwright, it was—'

'I want Stanley to explain.' Mom cut Jaxon off.

Holes? That's what she was worried about? She looked again at the spot where the hand stuck up from the ground. She looked directly at it, but her eyes whizzed past, like she didn't see anything but a few twigs stacked on the grass.

'We were being archanologists,' Miren said, hugging Mom's hip. 'I'm Stanley's assistant. His *official* assistant, like how Stanley used to help Daddy dig up dinos, and that—'

'Archaeologists,' Stanley interrupted. 'Like in *National Geographic*.' Stanley sighed. He could already tell Mom wouldn't understand, even if, by some miracle, she didn't notice the bones right in front of her. Worse, she flinched when Miren said the word 'Daddy', like just hearing it hurt.

'So you thought you could just dig up the garden? Do you know how much it's going to cost to fill all this in?' Her mouth tugged down at the edges.

'We can fill it in, Mom. I'm sorry. We didn't think about—'

'No, you weren't thinking.' Mom squeezed her eyes shut. 'Just go inside, Stanley. You can stay with Ms Francine while Miren and I go to the movies. I already bought three tickets, but I guess that money's just going to be wasted.'

'Woot! What are we going to see? Because I heard there's this new movie with Radish Redfern, that's Stripy Pony's best friend, and if so we have to see it.' Miren skipped around the garden, even though she had to gasp for air. 'Can Stanley come, too? Pleeease, Mom!'

'Not today, sweetie. Stanley can stay home and think about what he's done.'

'Mrs Stanwright, if I may,' Jaxon said. 'I think I might be able to explain. You see, it all started with the Darby Brothers' Mystery #148, *The Case of the Missing*—'

'Get in the car, Jaxon. I'll drop you off on the way to the movies.'

'Yes, Mrs Stanwright.'

They left Stanley alone in the garden. He slumped down next to the bone hand. He couldn't understand why his mother couldn't see it. Part of him was glad, because it meant he could keep digging, but the other part felt weird. Not just because he'd made her mad. There was something else, too. Kind of an itchy feeling behind his ears. Like the tickle he sometimes got when he was stopped at the top of a roller coaster waiting for the big plunge.

After a few minutes, the sky thundered and fat raindrops plopped on Stanley's head. He looked up as a finger of lightning streaked across the sky.

'Come inside,' called Ms Francine from the kitchen window. 'I made fresh bread to go with your borscht.'

Stanley ignored her. He picked up Miren's tiny shovel and went around the garden filling in the holes.

He watched the hand out of the corner of his eye as he worked. It stayed still, except when the wind blew hard and made the spindly bones shiver. Before he went in, he smoothed a thick layer of mud on top of the bones. Better safe than sorry. He closed the door, and when he peeked through the back window, lightning illuminated a single white knuckle already free of mud.

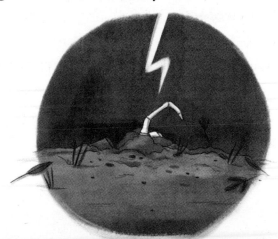

CHAPTER SEVEN

At midnight, Stanley padded into Miren's room and found her bed empty. He'd had a dream that she'd been crying, and he wanted to tell her he wasn't mad any more that she'd spilt his secret. Not that it had mattered.

Ms Francine stood by the back window, talking on the phone.

'Of course I'm sure. I can stay as long as you need. Don't worry about me and Stanley.' She pressed her face to the glass. Stanley couldn't see what she was looking at. 'What do you want me to tell him?'

Stanley tiptoed across the cool tiles and peeked into the living room.

'Ah, wait,' Ms Francine said without turning around. 'Here he is now. You can tell him yourself. Your momma,' she said, patting his head and handing him the phone.

'Mom, where are you? Where's Miren?'

'Stanley,' Mom said. Her voice sounded sticky and broken. 'I'm sorry about what I said earlier. I don't care about the garden.'

'I know,' Stanley said. 'It looks better now anyway, I fixed it. What's going on?'

'Your sister got sick at the movies, Stan, she couldn't . . . We had to go to the hospital, but don't worry, OK? Everything's going to be fine.'

'What kind of sick?' Stanley said, the sides of his mouth going numb. He remembered what he'd said earlier about wishing Miren would disappear, that she didn't even exist.

'We'll be home in the morning.' Mom drew in a sharp breath. 'Ms Francine said she'll bake you cookies for breakfast. The kind from the tube, your favourite.'

'Can I talk to Miren?'

'I have to go now, sweetheart. I love you. Be good for Ms Francine.'

'Mom!'

The line clicked off before Stanley could say goodbye.

Ms Francine peeled the phone from his hand and put it back on the charger.

'How about a midnight snack? We can eat hot cocoa with marshmallows and chocolate sauce.'

'No thanks,' Stanley said.

He pressed his face to the glass like Ms Francine had done. He saw the pieces of his camera lying forgotten in the grass. The hand flapped back and forth in the wind, the bones making a clicking sort of music. The mud he'd piled on top of them was gone.

'How come you can see it and my mom can't?'

Ms Francine closed a wrinkly hand around Stanley's shoulder.

'We see what we want to see,' said Ms Francine, and she went into the kitchen to boil water for the cocoa.

CHAPTER EIGHT

Miren squirmed as Mom slid the soft tubes into her nose the next morning at the dining table. She hadn't said anything all morning, not even when Stanley offered to pick the blueberries out of her blueberry pancakes.

'See, Miren just needs to breathe some fresh air for a while, then she'll feel all better. Right, baby?' Mom scooted aside a stack of old magazines to make room for Miren's new oxygen tank. It looked like the tank they used to blow up balloons at Party Dollar, only this one had a handle and wheels attached.

'Why does she need an oxygen tank to get fresh air anyway?' Stanley didn't understand anything that was happening. Why was Miren being so quiet?

'You need to hurry up or you'll miss the bus,' Mom said. She got up and stuffed her phone and a pack of tissues into her crackled blue bag.

'Mom!'

Stanley followed her to her room. She picked through the laundry piled on the armchair, searching for clean socks. She didn't even look up at him. She found a pair and then walked right past him back into the dining room.

'Call me if you need anything,' she was telling Ms Francine. 'I left Dr Cynthia's number on the fridge, and—'

'Mom!' Something inside Stanley cracked. Without Slurpy to keep him in check, his anger bubbled up quickly, swirling around his stomach like a volcano. 'I need you to tell me the truth!'

He was so frustrated he could've punched a hole in the dining room table, but instead he started to cry. Big, stupid tears that burned his cheeks. Mom folded her arms around him, trying to make him feel better, but he just kept crying. Like he really was a volcano, and everything he'd been holding inside was erupting.

'Your sister's going to be fine, Stanley.'

'How do you know that?' he said between sobs.

Mom held him for so long he ran out of tears and ended up with a salty face and a sore throat. 'I think I hear the bus coming. Can you make it in time?' She released him, and he saw that her cheeks were wet, too.

'I guess,' he said, even though she still hadn't answered his question.

He pulled on his backpack and Miren's face crumpled. She'd been kind of stunned during the whole sob fest thing, but now she looked ready to explode, too. 'I want Stanley to stay with me. Mom, you have to let him!'

'Sweetheart, Stanley has to go to school.' Mom pulled them both into a hug. To Stanley's surprise, Miren didn't cry. The anger kind of oozed out of her, like she was too tired to even throw a tantrum. 'I'm so sorry, baby.' Mom looked at Miren for a long time, at the tubes stretching over her ears and into her nostrils and at the way her bottom lip kept tugging downward. Finally, she sighed and said, 'Well, maybe just for today.'

'Yes!' Miren said, some of her usual enthusiasm returning. 'Stanley and I are going on an adventure, right, Butt-Breath? Only I can't tell you about it, because it's a secret.'

'Not too much of an adventure, I hope,' Mom said. 'And sweetie, try not to call your brother Butt-Breath.'

She kissed Miren and Stanley on their foreheads and then left for work.

'What is this adventure I hear about?' Ms Francine said. She smelt like coconut and her hair was wet from the shower. Sometimes, if Mom worked really late, or if something happened like Miren getting sick, Ms Francine stayed overnight.

'Nothing,' Stanley said.

'Nothing,' echoed Miren. He could tell it was causing Miren physical pain to keep quiet.

'Well, if this nothing has to do with the hand flapping in the wind last night, you might go take a look.' She stared out of the window like she was remembering something sad and happy all at once. 'It grows faster than you think, this kind of tree. Especially with all that rain.'

Stanley looked at Miren. Her mouth dropped open.

Miren leapt out of her seat and started for the door. 'Last one to—' The tubes caught in her nose and pulled her backwards. She hit the ground, hard, and the tank tumbled after her, cracking on to the tiles.

Miren lay still for a second, a rag doll with the stuffing pulled out, and then her face turned red and her whole body started to shake. Ms Francine scooped her up and let her cry and scream into her shoulder. Stanley smoothed the hair out of her mouth and eyes.

After a while, Miren's cries turned to heaves and she stopped shaking. Stanley thought that meant she felt better, because she wasn't sobbing any more, but then her lungs started to make these terrible scratchy noises. All the pink drained from her face, and she was gasping for air. Quickly, Ms Francine pressed the tubes back into her nose.

The scratchy sounds died away. Stanley rubbed Miren's shoulder and wished things could go back to how they were before, when Miren was a baby and her biggest problem was a dirty nappy or a scraped knee. The three of them sat on the kitchen floor like that for a while, until Miren turned pink again and her breathing sounded normal. Stanley picked at a peeling vinyl tile. He still remembered the day she'd tripped over it and broken her little finger. He'd thought that was the worst thing that would ever happen to her, but now . . . now he didn't know what to think.

'Maybe little one will take a rest. What do you say, little one?'

Miren balled up her fists. 'I'm not little,' she said, her voice ragged. 'And I don't need a nap.'

'Very well.'

Ms Francine carried Miren and her tank into the garden. A breeze ruffled Stanley's hair. He didn't understand why it was better to get air from a machine than from outside, but he could see now that Miren really was sick.

He stopped dead a few feet away from the bone hand. Ms Francine had been right. It wasn't just a hand any more. Miren wiggled free of Ms Francine's grasp.

'Slowly, little girl. You will run out of air if you move so fast.'

A skeletal arm stretched up from the ground, fingers curled into a claw, like they were trying to snatch a cloud from the sky. Stanley stopped, and for a moment he could almost feel those bony fingers reaching down his throat. That itchy feeling snaked its way under his skin again, too. Not afraid, not really, just waiting.

Then he remembered about the camera, and the tingling went away and a sour taste filled his mouth. If Miren hadn't broken it, he could've snapped a shot right now that might have won him the Young Discoverer's Prize. Dad would have gone on the trip with him, and maybe he'd see what he was missing and decide to come home and take care of him and

Miren like he was supposed to.

But he couldn't think about that now. Not when Miren was so sick. How could he be mad at her when she couldn't even breathe by herself? Like it or not, the contest would have to wait.

Miren tiptoed right up to the arm and pinched the bony thumb. White fingers closed around her fist. Stanley lunged forward to help her, but she laughed and said, 'Hey! That tickles.'

She eased her fingers free, and the hand twisted around to form a thumbs-up. Miren clapped and giggled and snorted, just like the time they saw the seals dancing at SeaWorld. Ms Francine patted her eyes and looked at the arm like it was an old friend.

'We should water it,' Miren said. Her voice sounded all weird and far away, and it gave Stanley the creeps.

But Miren was sick, and even though she was annoying, Stanley realized he would do anything to make her feel better.

Even if it was super spooky.

He helped Miren fill a coffee tin with water and pour it at the base of the bone. They sat and watched to see if the skeleton would grow again. The whole time, Stanley's mind reeled. He had so many new facts, impossible facts, that he didn't know where to put them all. Like that time he tried to run too many games at once and his computer crashed. That was how his brain felt.

At lunchtime, Ms Francine brought them cucumber salad served in coffee mugs. They ate the crunchy salad and washed it down with glasses of iced mint tea. Stanley stacked the dishes inside the empty coffee tin.

He looked up when he was done and saw the skeleton arm quiver. It started at the base, like a tiny earthquake, and shot all the way up to the bony fingers. He let the tin of dishes he'd been holding fall with a clunk on to the grass. Miren jumped and shouted and pointed as a shoulder blade pushed up through the mud, followed by a rib and the top part of a skull.

She jumped so much her breath got scratchy, and Stanley had to make her sit down next to him in the grass. He put his arms around her to keep her still, but in the end he was the one who was shaking.

They watched the skeleton closely for the rest of the day, Stanley too stunned to say much, Miren talking non-stop about how the skeleton was awesome and how he was going to be her new best friend.

Stanley wasn't so sure about that. The same frozen, itchy fingers curled around his lungs and squeezed. He remembered the feeling he'd had when he first saw the bone, like nothing would ever be the same again. The bone had changed things, and no matter how hard he might try, he could never go back to before.

Before Miren got sick, or before the bone started to grow.

'Stanley, are you even listening to me? I said, what type of gift do you give a skeleton for Christmas? I mean, it's not for a while and everything, but I was thinking about a coat, because it's probably cold not having skin . . . or maybe a new pair of tap shoes!'

'Why would you give tap shoes to a skeleton?' Stanley said, so dazed he was hardly listening.

'They're for dancing, duh, don't you know anything?'

Miren went on like that until the sun dipped behind the fence, casting the shed and the shrubs and the bones in a blazing gold glow. 'Dinnertime!' called Ms Francine from inside the house. Her voice was so big she didn't even need to open a window, which was good, because otherwise Stanley might not have heard her. His brain felt about a million miles away.

Stanley helped Miren inside, and they ate potato

soup and hard rolls for dinner. At least it wasn't borscht.

Mom came home from work before the sun had even gone down for the day. Ms Francine heated up soup and they all sat around the dining table, talking about their day. Stanley tried to keep up his end of the conversation, but his thoughts kept drifting back to the bones.

He must have zoned out for a while, because suddenly he heard Miren say, 'And, next thing I knew, it made a thumbs-up, like this.' As soon as she said it, she clapped a hand over her mouth. 'Sorry, Stanley.' There must be something in little kid DNA that makes it impossible for them not to blab.

'What made a thumbs-up?' Mom said.

Miren thought about it for a long time. 'Oh, nothing. It was just this dumb TV show Stanley made me watch.'

Mom laughed and ruffled Miren's hair. Stanley had to admit he was kind of impressed with her answer. Who knew she could be such a good liar? 'You'll have to let me watch it sometime. Promise?'

'OK,' Miren said. 'One day.'

After that, Ms Francine went home and Mom put Miren to bed. She always sat with her and read stories from Miren's favourite book, all about a stinky block of cheese.

Stanley sat at the dinner table, doing his homework. Outside, the moon rose big and orange in the sky, like a Halloween pumpkin.

Stanley couldn't wait till Halloween. He was going to be Dagger Rockbomb, and Jaxon was going as BrainBlaster 2000, this zombie robot boss with spinning eyeballs and lasers shooting out of his tongue. Jaxon's dad was this special effects guru. Every year he turned his whole garden into a haunted house and had a huge party for the entire neighbourhood. It was going to be epic, even if it was the same day as Miren's birthday.

Mom poured a glass of wine and went outside to talk on the phone. Stanley was pretty sure she was calling Dad. Maybe this time he would answer, and then Mom could put Stanley on the phone, too, instead of leaving another message. Maybe, but knowing Dad, probably not.

While the phone was ringing, Mom walked right up to the skeleton arm a bunch of times without ever looking down at it. But that wasn't the weirdest part. At one point, she stepped right through it, like it wasn't even there, like the arm was made of smoke instead of bone. Stanley couldn't understand it.

'I told Dad you say hi,' Mom said a few seconds

later when she came inside.

'I could have told him myself,' Stanley said, an acidy taste settling on the back of his tongue. 'Why doesn't he ever pick up his phone any more?'

'You know he's busy with his new job. We talked about this.'

'Yeah, whatever.'

Mom snapped her phone shut and set it on the counter. 'I told him Miren's going to be fine. Kids need oxygen all the time, even some kids who just have colds, I looked it up online. Anyway, I'm sure he'll call back in the morning.' Mom dragged her fingernails across her forehead. 'And, like I said, Miren just needs a little rest. If it was anything serious, he'd—'

'What? If what was anything serious?'

'Nothing, just don't be so hard on your dad, OK?'

Stanley didn't say anything for a while. Suddenly, he didn't feel like talking about Dad any more.

'You'd better go to bed, sweetheart, so you're not tired tomorrow.'

'Can't I stay home from school again? Someone has to be here to take care of Miren.' The words came out before he could stop them.

Mom got a look on her face like he'd hit her, but

then she turned it into a smile. 'Ms Francine will be here, and you've already missed enough school.'

'But Miren needs me.' Also, a tiny part of him was hoping to spend the day digging. All he had to do was find a camera and get the perfect shot. Then Dad would come on the trip with him, and he'd remember how great it was when he'd lived at home, and he'd give up his stupid job in California. Dad might not be perfect, but things had been better when he was here. It was a fact.

Mom thought about it for a long time. Her fingers moved down from her forehead and started rubbing her jaw. 'We can stop by McDonald's on the way to school, how about that? I'll drive you. Meet me at the car at six thirty. Deal?'

Stanley wanted to argue, but Mom looked so tired he couldn't bring himself to do it. 'Deal.'

'Goodnight, Stanley.' She hugged him for so long his shoulders started to ache.

'Goodnight, Mom.' He watched her stare out of the darkened window. Her eyes fell on the bone arm once, twice. The third time, her forehead creased and she opened her mouth, like she wanted to say something, but a moment later she closed it again.

'Don't let the wully bugs bite,' he added.

He waited for her to answer, but she just kept staring out of the window, like maybe there was something there other than the bone. Something she could see and Stanley couldn't.

CHAPTER NINE

Things were better in the morning, and the day after that. On Friday, Stanley got to go to Jaxon's house after school. Jaxon was so hopped up on sugar from eating a whole plate of double fudge cookies, they didn't even have to count fence slats before they started playing *Ancient Aliens Attack!*

'So, I've been thinking,' Jaxon said as he torpedoed an ancient alien dressed like King Tut, 'about the Young Discoverer's Prize.' Stanley had been thinking about it, too. They only had one week to get the perfect picture. 'We should start keeping a record of how fast the skeleton grows. With charts and stuff. Scientists love charts, and then we'll be sure to win.'

'Yeah,' Stanley said, 'but I don't have a camera. Mrs Hammelstein said hers was broken, and Principal Eaks said I couldn't borrow the school's unless it was for homework.'

'No worries, I'll sleep over this weekend and we can take pictures with my iPad.' Jaxon shrugged, like it was no big deal. 'I already asked my mom and she said it's OK.'

Out of nowhere, the victory music soundtrack from *Skatepark Zombie Death Bash* blasted in Stanley's head.

'Your iPad? Why didn't I think of that?'

'Because you never wrote out a checklist like I told you? In one column, you put—'

'No, because you're a genius! A real-life, genuine superhero sidekick.'

'Sidekick?'

———

Later that night, Mom picked up Stanley and Jaxon, and they went to Lazlo's Pizza and Mini-Golf. Stanley used to love going there when he was a kid, but what he really wanted was to get home and take a picture of the skeleton. Miren sat in the front seat, so Stanley and

Jaxon could sit together in the back. The oxygen tank rolled around in the boot. On Thursday, the doctor said she didn't have to wear it any more, unless she felt like she needed it.

'I want to get a snow-cone and an ice cream and one of those lollipops with the swirly part in the middle.' Miren bounced in her seat. 'And Ashleigh wants a hot dog, or maybe a burrito. She can't decide.'

'Ashleigh can't eat,' Jaxon said. 'She's a doll.'

Also, only babies carry dolls, Stanley wanted to say but didn't.

Miren twisted around in her seat and shook her head at Jaxon. 'Oh really, smarty-pants? If she can't eat, then how come she knows how to potty?'

Miren squeezed Ashleigh's tummy, and the doll piddled all over Jaxon's knee. Stanley laughed so hard he swallowed his cinnamon gum. Mom kept driving and pretended not to notice. He knew she was just happy to see Miren feeling better.

At the snack shack, Mom ordered an ice cream for Miren and a hot dog for Baby Ashleigh. Seriously, she wasted money on food for a doll. Stanley and Jaxon shared purple candyfloss and a burrito.

Miren, Ashleigh, and Mom won at mini-golf.

Mostly because Stanley let them win. Also, Jaxon was terrible at putting. He kept getting distracted because of this squiggly mark on his ball that looked like a hair.

After that, Mom took Miren to play on the slides, and Stanley and Jaxon found an arcade version of *PixelBlock*. Only twenty-five cents a game. Ms Francine had given Stanley enough quarters to play all night, and maybe the next day, too.

'Don't tell Momma,' she said that morning before school. 'Go have fun with your friend. Little boys don't have enough fun these days. Not like when I was in Kyrgyzstan.'

'Oh my god, zombie chicken at five o'clock. Run, Stanley!'

Stanley smashed the controls as fast as he could, but it was too late. The zombie chicken exploded and destroyed the space portal they'd built with the last of their moonstone.

'Ugh, I hate this game. Let's go get some pizza, then we can play *World War 2½: Land of the Undead*.'

'Sounds goo—'

Miren came out of nowhere and cannonballed into Stanley's stomach.

'We rode the slides, and Ashleigh went first, and her

head fell off, but the man at the desk, his name was Carl, put it back on with superglue, so now she's not beheaded any more!' Miren held up her doll for Stanley to inspect.

'Nope, definitely not beheaded,' Stanley said, patting Ashleigh gingerly on the scalp. 'What do you say we get some pizza?'

'Large pepperoni, sauce on the side?' Mom said.

'Yes, please.' Jaxon bit his lip. 'Sorry, I just don't like thinking about the sauce hiding under all that cheese. You know, I like to see what I eat.'

'You're one strange cookie.' Stanley punched Jaxon's shoulder. Some kids at school thought Jaxon was weird for saying things like that, but Stanley knew better. The problem was, he was too smart for his own good. 'Let's go get a table. Come on.' They raced through the aisles, looking for an empty booth.

'Save a seat for Ashleigh,' Miren called after them.

The pizza tasted better than any Stanley remembered, even though the sauce came in a cup instead of under the cheese like it was supposed to. Miren ate half a piece of pizza and drank two mega-size Diet Cokes.

Stanley was surprised when she fell asleep on the car ride home, after all that caffeine. Mom stopped by Jaxon's house to pick up his things.

'This is going to be the most epic sleepover weekend in history,' Jaxon said while their moms stood in the driveway, talking. 'It's just like Darby Brothers' Mystery #57, *The Case of the Dancing Bones*.'

'Is this another dead cat story?' Stanley said.

'No, listen. James and Oliver spend the night in the cemetery, and they see what looks like a dancing skeleton, only it's really the groundskeeper wearing a costume to scare away grave robbers.'

'How is that anything like anything?'

'Don't you see? You've got a dancing skeleton, too, sort of. Only it's not just some guy wearing a costume. It's real.' Jaxon took his iPad from his backpack. 'And we're going to prove it.'

CHAPTER TEN

That night, Stanley and Jaxon snuck into the garden after everyone had gone to sleep. Mom's fork and spoon wind chime clinked in the chilly air. Jaxon took a deep breath and switched on the torch he always kept in his Darby Brothers' Just-in-Case investigator's backpack.

The beam lit on a bony rib cage sticking straight up out of the ground. The skeleton's hands covered his face, like maybe he was shielding his eyes from the light. Stanley peered through his ribs at the fence beyond, and then he ran a shaky finger along the skeleton's sternum.

'Smooth,' Stanley said. 'Shouldn't it be, I don't know, messier?'

'Let me see,' Jaxon said, sounding

braver than he looked.

He took a magnifying glass from his pack and scanned the stubby vertebrae and fragile finger bones.

'Ouch!' Jaxon fell back on his butt, clutching his nose.

'What happened?'

'He flicked me!'

'What?' Stanley pressed his nose close to the skeleton's face, and sure enough, a bony finger shot out and hit him in the left nostril.

'Hey!' Stanley backed up, tripped over Jaxon's legs, and dropped to the grass beside him.

'That is not natural,' said Jaxon, dragging himself back towards the house.

'Wait,' said Stanley, standing up and brushing himself off. He wasn't going to let a little flick stop him now. 'Think of it like we're scientists discovering a new species. *Skeletus animatus*, get it – the moving skeleton?' Stanley was trying to make a joke, but inside his stomach had twisted into a big, tingly knot.

'That's not how you say it in Latin.' Jaxon stood up, too, but he didn't look like he wanted to come near the skeleton again.

Stanley groaned. 'Whatever, look, the point is, no

one's ever seen anything like this. If we get a picture, we could be famous. Not just the Young Discoverer's Prize. We could be on TV and stuff.' And maybe then Dad would answer his phone when Mom called.

'Fine, let's just take a picture and get out of here,' said Jaxon, a drop of blood trickling from his nose.

'No, hold on.' Why hadn't Stanley thought of it before? 'I've got a better idea. Let's take a video. If we send that in as our entry, there's no way we can lose.'

Jaxon fished the iPad from his backpack and aimed it at the skeleton's torso. His hands were still shaking, but Stanley didn't say anything. Inside, he felt the same way.

'Say cheese,' Stanley said. Jaxon didn't laugh.

The skeleton crumpled forward as soon as the iPad started recording, wrapping his arms over his head and curling into a tiny ball.

'Not cool,' Jaxon said, nearly dropping the iPad. 'All I got was a blur.'

'Let me see.' Stanley played back the video. Sure enough, all he could see was a white light sweeping across the screen, kind of like the beam of a torch. 'Here, let me do it.' He tried to sound brave, but really he had to swallow hard to keep from throwing up.

Stanley waited for the skeleton to stretch back to its full height, but it didn't move . . . at first. Not until Stanley and Jaxon turned their backs and closed their eyes. Then, they heard bones clinking together, and when they turned around the skeleton was upright again.

'I wish he'd take his hands away from his eyes,' said Stanley, although his tongue had gone numb, and if the skeleton had moved his hands at that exact moment he might have screamed.

'Just take the video so we can go inside.' Jaxon twisted his shirt in his hands and counted under his breath.

'OK, here it goes.'

Stanley zoomed in and pressed the button. The skeleton collapsed to one side again, so that all Stanley captured was a long, white blur.

'I don't think he wants to be on camera,' Jaxon said. 'Oh my god, what am I saying? Skeletons don't want anything. Stanley, you know I'm your friend, right? But can we please go inside?'

Stanley wasn't listening. He was determined to make this happen, whether the skeleton wanted it to or not. 'Maybe the shutter speed's too slow or something.' Stanley didn't know what that meant, but it sounded good. 'Let's try to snap a regular picture.'

'I'm leaving, OK? Hold on to the iPad, I'm out of here.'

'Not yet,' Stanley said, but Jaxon had already started towards the door.

Stanley didn't want Jaxon to be mad at him, but he *had* to get a good shot. Jaxon might not need to win the prize, but he did. Especially now that Miren was really sick. If he won the trip, he could convince Dad to come home, and then things would be how they used to be. Dad could get a job at a law firm in town, Mom could quit at Walgreens and go to dog grooming school, and they wouldn't have to worry about bills all the time. Dad was like the hard drive to the Stanwright family computer. With him gone, they were just a bunch of spare parts.

Stanley did everything he could think of to snap a clear picture of the skeleton growing in his garden. He pretended to be cleaning the iPad's screen, and then he swung around for a surprise shot. Nothing but blur. He hid the iPad behind his back and then slid it out so fast no normal person would have had time to react.

The skeleton seemed to know each move he was going to make before he made it.

'You win,' Stanley said after the tenth failed shot. 'Guess I'll go back inside.'

Stanley strolled across the garden, humming, and closed the door behind him. Quick as a cat, he ducked under the window, held up the iPad, and clicked.

Heart banging against his ribs, he lowered the iPad and looked at the photo he had taken. The top part of a skeleton stared back at him. Jaw open. Two cavern eyes gaping like endless black holes, hungry and swirling.

But that wasn't the weird part. The skeleton's body was draped in velvety black fabric that reflected back the light. A hood hung low over his forehead, casting long shadows down his cheeks. And one bony finger pointed at the house. Not at Stanley, but off to his left.

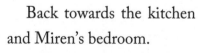

Back towards the kitchen and Miren's bedroom.

'Did you get one?' Jaxon said when Stanley plopped down on his bed. Jaxon was playing *PixelBlock* on Stanley's ancient computer. 'Let me see.'

Bitter liquid coated Stanley's throat.

He turned the iPad around to show Jaxon, but even as he did, the image changed, like one of those sand paintings that go fuzzy when you shake them.

'I think you were right,' Stanley said, the words scratching the inside of his mouth. 'He doesn't want to have his picture taken.'

CHAPTER ELEVEN

Miren bounced up and down in her seat at the dining table, the chair legs creaking under her weight.

'This is why little ones shouldn't eat coffee for breakfast,' Ms Francine said.

'She only had one sip,' said Stanley.

'And I'm not little!'

'Eat your biscuits, not-little girl. It will help soak up some of that energy.'

'Ashleigh and I want to go visit Princy after breakfast,' said Miren. 'He's got so big, soon he'll be as tall as me, and we're going to play hide-and-seek and freeze tag. He told me so.'

'Ah yes. These trees grow fast,' Ms Francine said, shaking her head. She closed her hands over the silver locket she always wore around her neck.

'Wait a minute, who's Princy?' Jaxon said.

'The skeleton, dumb-dumb! I call him Princy because

he has those puffy sleeves and that shiny gold hat. Oh, and he lives in this huge castle where everyone dances all the time and drinks tea from fancy cups. But really, he doesn't have a name.'

Stanley and Jaxon looked at each other. Ms Francine laughed.

'What did I tell you?' she said. 'We see what we want to see.'

An image of a skeleton in a crinkly black cloak floated behind Stanley's eyes. He shook his head to make it go away, but it stuck there. Like someone had sealed his ears shut with superglue.

After breakfast, Stanley and Miren went outside and watered Princy. Stanley would have rather been taking photos, but he suspected Jaxon had given up on his idea of trying to document the skeleton's growth. Why else would he have volunteered to stay inside and help Ms Francine with the dishes? Oh well, it didn't matter anyway. At this rate, there was no way he was going to win the Young Discoverer's Prize. Not if every photo he took disappeared.

While Stanley and Miren sat watching and sipping frozen orange juice from a can, the skeleton started to rumble. It heaved and trembled, and then the top part of a pelvis broke through the mud. Stanley froze in place, heart getting pinched between his ribs.

Beside him, Miren jumped up and punched the sky. 'You can do it, Princy!'

She flung her arms around the skeleton's rib cage. Stanley was sure the brittle bones would crack under her weight, but they didn't. Instead, the skeleton peeled its hands away from its face and patted Miren's back.

In the daylight, the skeleton's eye sockets didn't look quite as black and swirly as they had the night before, but they still reminded Stanley of caves. Caves that went on and on without end. He didn't see any sign of the black cloak, either.

That part weirded him out more than anything. How could something be there one minute and then disappear the next? Like it had never even existed? Probably because he'd imagined the whole creepy cloak thing in the first place.

'Just one more bucket, please!' Miren said for maybe the hundredth time.

Princy had gone still after patting Miren's back, and she was determined to make him move again. Stanley wanted to go inside and talk Jaxon into helping him take more photos, but Miren looked so skinny and sick in her Stripy Pony nightgown, he couldn't say no.

'Fine, just one more.'

Miren and Stanley poured bucket after bucket of water on to the skeleton and waited. By eleven, it had grown two more inches. Now, whenever the wind brushed past, the bones made a sound like branches rattling on a dead tree. Maybe it *was* a tree, like Ms Francine said. Only this one was made of bone instead of wood.

'Lunchtime!' Jaxon called later from the kitchen window. 'Cookies and cucumber sandwiches.'

Stanley helped Miren inside, shocked at how much time had passed. She was so sleepy after all the watering that Ms Francine put her to bed. She couldn't even stay awake long enough for lunch. After that, Stanley ate his cookies in silence, feeling bad for leaving Jaxon alone with Ms Francine on their super sleepover weekend and confused about the bones.

'Maybe we should play some *Ancient Aliens Attack!*' Stanley said when he'd devoured his last cookie. 'You can show me that moon fort you built that looks like a bologna sandwich.'

'I've got a better idea,' Jaxon said, peering at the bones through the picture window. 'Sorry I acted like such a wuss last night.'

'What? You didn't, it's fine.'

'No.' He swallowed a lump of cucumber sandwich. 'I know how much you want to win that prize. And . . . I think we should try again.'

'Are you sure?' Stanley said, half hoping he was kidding. He wanted more than anything to see his dad, but he was also really freaked out.

'Yeah.' Jaxon spent a long time dusting all of the crumbs from his plate on to his napkin. 'I'm sure.'

After lunch, they went back outside, iPad at the ready. Stanley could tell Jaxon was trying to be brave for him. He kept giving the skeleton funny looks, but he never once said he was scared.

'Maybe if you take a picture from behind, he won't have time to duck,' Jaxon said. He handed Stanley the iPad, his hands only shaking a little. 'I'll distract him.'

Jaxon waved his arms around and shouted out stuff like, 'Hey, you big bag of bones, over here!'

Stanley got into position and lined up his shot.

Everything looked normal through the lens. He held his finger over the button. He was about to press down when the image with the cloak crept into his head. Suddenly, his stomach went all wobbly and he wished he hadn't eaten so many cookies. Maybe he should have told Jaxon about the cloak. But no, that was stupid. The cloak wasn't even real.

'Did you get one?' Jaxon called. 'My arms are getting tired.'

'Just a sec!' Stanley pressed the button, and the iPad counted down and then made that little shutter noise.

'What's it look like?' Jaxon ran up behind Stanley, and they both stared at the picture they had captured. Before it could change, Stanley made a copy and saved it to the home screen. It was the back of a skeleton, poking halfway up out of the ground. There was no cloak and no creepy, cavern eyes. Relief washed over Stanley's skin.

'Whoa, what's that?' Jaxon said, backing away from the screen.

'What?' Stanley looked closer. In the picture, there was something glittering in the grass near the skeleton's pelvis. A long, curved blade.

'That's it, I'm out of here. Sorry, Stanley!' Jaxon's eyes lingered for a moment on the grass. In real life, not in the photo. 'It doesn't make any sense,' he said under his breath.

Stanley followed his gaze, a cool wind snaking up his T-shirt. Jaxon was right; it didn't make sense. No matter how hard he looked, he kept coming to the same conclusion.

In the photo, he could see the blade reflecting back the light from the iPad's screen. But when he lowered the tablet and looked at the ground right in front of him, there was nothing. Just mud and shadows and dark green grass tickling white-washed bones.

CHAPTER TWELVE

Rain battered the roof and made the lights flicker, like any minute the power might go out.

'I'm just saying, it's creepy.' Jaxon counted to five over and over while he waited for Stanley's computer to load. 'People will think it's a prank.'

'Yeah, maybe.' Stanley dragged a bucket from the garage and put it under the leak next to his bed.

'Might as well wait till you get a better shot. One people will take seriously, right?'

Stanley didn't answer. It was one thing for Jaxon to wait; the contest was just fun and games for him, but for Stanley it was different.

'Hey, look at this,' Jaxon said, half standing and banging his knees on Stanley's keyboard. 'There are already some entries for the Young Discoverer's Prize online. Check it out.'

'Online?'

'Yeah, people post entries on the website, and kids from all over the world can like them or leave comments.'

'Are you serious? Let's see.'

Jaxon clicked the link. As usual, Stanley's old PC took ages to load.

'This first kid found a shark tooth buried on a beach in Florida,' Jaxon said, scanning through the pixelated photos. 'He already has fifty-two likes.'

'What? How can we ever catch up to that? And that's not even a real discovery; it probably came off somebody's necklace.'

'Hang on, look at this.' Jaxon clicked on the next entry. The photograph showed a boy holding up what looked like a leg. 'Dinosaur bone, uncovered in the Sahara Desert.'

'That could have come from a baby dinosaur, I guess,' said Stanley, not impressed. 'One hundred and twenty-five likes! What is wrong with people? It's probably not even from a real dinosaur. I bet it's a camel or something.'

Jaxon scrolled through the rest of the entries. Thirteen so far. When he reached the bottom, he got a mysterious look on his face. It was the same half smile he got whenever he was reading one of his Darby Brothers' mysteries.

'You know,' he said, weighing his words, 'your picture might be weird, but it's definitely more interesting than any of these.'

'I thought you said people will think it's a prank?'

'Maybe, but none of the others include growth charts or notes. I mean, it's probably a crazy idea, but—'

That was all Stanley needed to hear. He grabbed Jaxon's iPad and pulled up the submission form for the Young Discoverer's Prize.

'Hold it, I didn't mean we should submit it right now. We don't have our notes ready.'

'We can get them ready.' Stanley typed in his information as he was talking. 'Look, you can keep adding to your entry until the deadline. We might as well post it now, so we can get as many likes as possible.'

'I don't know . . .'

Stanley uploaded the photo. There was only one box left to fill out. 'What should we call our entry? If we say it's a human skeleton, won't they send the police or something?'

'Holy crab cakes, Stanley! I can't believe this didn't

occur to me sooner. If someone sees a picture of a dead human body in your garden, what are they going to think?'

Stanley shrugged. He was willing to take that risk.

'Forget about pranks,' Jaxon said. 'They're going to think you're a murderer, that's what. This is just like Darby Brothers' Mystery #17, *The Accidental Frame-Up*.'

'Enough with the Darby Brothers already.'

'Fine, I'm just saying, I've changed my mind. Posting this picture is a bad idea. A dangerous idea.'

Stanley nodded, but while Jaxon had been talking he'd already typed out *'Skeletus animatus'* in the final box. The iPad made a whooshing sound as he pressed the submit button.

'Tell me you didn't just do that.'

Jaxon lunged for the iPad, but he was too late. They both watched as, before their eyes, a new entry popped on to the big monitor.

Posted at 1:59 p.m., *Skeletus animatus*.

A bolt of lightning flashed outside the window. As it did, Stanley's stomach twisted into a knot, like there was a clown inside him trying to turn his guts into balloon animals. Maybe Jaxon was right. Maybe the police would come pounding on his door, shouting –

'Time for hot cocoa!' Ms Francine burst into the room, making Stanley drop the iPad and almost pee his pants. 'I added a pinch of salt, just the way you like it.' She tilted her head at Stanley. 'Why so frightened, little Stanley? It's only a thunderstorm. In Kyrgyzstan, we would pray for lightning like this to come down and melt all the snow.' She wiggled her bushy eyebrows at him. When he still didn't move, she picked him up by the collar and hoisted him into the hall. 'Come on, my wee goats, let's eat!'

'You can't eat cocoa,' Stanley said after he'd been forced into a seat at the dining table. 'Besides, we were busy doing stuff. At least let me go get the iPad.' Ms Francine ignored him. She poured each of them a cup of thick hot chocolate topped with marshmallows.

They ate in silence, Jaxon and Stanley at the table, Ms Francine sitting on the windowsill. She twirled her locket in her clawed hand and stared outside, where the skeleton tree swayed back and forth in the wind.

'Who's in your locket?' Jaxon said after a while, blowing on his cocoa. It was clear they weren't going to get out of this without making a little conversation. 'Can I see?'

'Smart boy. How do you know I keep someone hidden in there?'

'People always keep important pictures in lockets. Like in this one Darby Brothers' mystery, where James and Oliver's grandma—'

'You talk a lot about these Darby Brothers. What makes them so great? You have mysteries, too.' Ms Francine batted a hand at the skeleton. 'You can solve them without this James and Oliver.'

'Yeah, but—'

'Take some advice from an old woman. Live the life you have, because one day. Poof! You won't have it any more.'

She opened up the locket and showed them a black-and-white picture of a baby on one side, and a man with a bristly moustache and a fuzzy hat on the other.

'Papa died when I was three or four.'

'You don't remember which one?' Jaxon said.

'Three or four might not seem like so long ago when you are little, but try telling them apart when you're as old as me.' She flicked the side of her crooked nose. 'Papa passed away in his favourite chair. He was playing chess, and I sat in the windowsill, watching. I loved to watch Papa play chess. The way the line in between his brow would crease.'

'Who was he playing?' Stanley said.

Ms Francine shrugged. 'You know, this one and that one.'

'You don't remember that, either?' Jaxon said.

'Maybe I do, maybe I don't.'

Stanley watched the way her eyes lingered on the skeleton. A tear rolled down her cheek.

'You will see,' Ms Francine said, and she clanked her empty mug on the metal tray.

'Where's Miren anyway?' Stanley said.

'Ah yes, little Miren is tired after so much excitement. I went to wake her up, and you know what she said?' Stanley shook his head. '"Go away, it's the day of the royal ball and Princy is about to serve tea."'

'She said that?' Jaxon said.

'Well, come to think of it, it was hard to tell with all the snoring.'

Jaxon offered to help clean up the dishes once they'd finished their cocoa – he was always annoyingly polite like that – but Ms Francine shooed them back to Stanley's room. 'Go, have fun. Let the old lady do the cleaning.'

'Finally,' said Stanley once they were back in his

room. 'Let's see if anyone liked the photo yet. Then, when we're done, we can make those charts you were talking about.'

Jaxon didn't answer. He was too busy staring at something on the floor.

'What is – ?' Stanley started, but then he saw the muddy footprints leading from the window to the bed. And that wasn't all. There was a wet handprint on Stanley's *PixelBlock* pillow. In the exact spot where Jaxon's iPad had been just a few minutes before.

CHAPTER THIRTEEN

They spent all day Sunday searching for Jaxon's iPad. The power went out three times, which didn't help. Even worse, Miren insisted on searching, too, which meant she mostly dragged Stanley around the house, telling him dumb stories about kids in her class Stanley had never met.

'And then Isaac, that's the one who eats bogeys, sent a letter to Natalie saying how he really liked her new shoes, the ones that light up and have wheels, but Natalie hates Isaac, because of the bogeys, and so she threw it away, and Isaac found it in the bin, and he cried so much Miss Gadd had to call the nurse.'

'Uh-huh,' said Stanley.

And to top it all off, it was raining so hard they couldn't even search outside.

'How could you lose an iPad?'

Mom said after she'd dropped Jaxon off at home later that night. 'I told Deb we'd pay for it, by the way.'

'But, Mom—'

'What else could I say?' Mom gnawed her bottom lip. 'Look, I know you didn't mean to, but you're almost a teenager, and I expect you to be more responsible than this. Especially –' Her voice got all crackly and she stopped talking.

Stanley wanted to tell her about the footprints, but he couldn't spill his secret. Not when he was so close.

She drove in silence the rest of the way home. When he got out of the car, it was so dark Stanley could barely see to get inside. Mom still hadn't replaced the bulb that burned out in the garage door opener. 'I'll find it, Mom, I promise.'

At first, he wasn't sure Mom had heard. Then she found him in the dark and pulled him close. Her wet cheeks pressed against his. She held him like that for a breathless moment, and then she went inside to run water for Miren's bath.

Later that night, Stanley had logged on to play *PixelBlock* when he saw a message from Jaxon flashing at the bottom of the screen.

Check out the Young Discoverer's website.
NOW!!!

Ants skittered from the top of Stanley's head all the way down his spine, or at least that was what it felt like. He typed in the web address and waited for the page to load. If only his computer wasn't some relic from a hundred years ago.

Finally, the picture of a boy holding a dinosaur tooth from the ad came together pixel by pixel. He didn't see anything new on the home page, so he clicked on the link to view the entries.

He half yelped, half laughed as soon as the screen loaded. Out of twenty-seven entries, *Skeletus animatus* was number one. It already had 341 likes, and it'd been on the site for less than a day. Stanley could already imagine what it would be like when he called Dad and told him he'd won the contest. Then later, on the plane ride home from their awesome trip, Dad would turn to him and say, 'I'm sorry, buddy, for being such an idiot.

I'm coming home.' Only it would sound better than that, because Dad always knew just how to put things. Because it would be real.

DARBYFAN#1: Can you believe it????? We're sure to win now!

STANTHEMAN64: No way! How did it happen so fast?

DARBYFAN#1: Read the comments section!

Stanley scrolled down and was amazed to find fifty-three comments from people all over the world.

DINOLOPOLIS20: What an amazing find! I've never seen anything like it.

TEAMDIGBOTS: Incredible! I mean, it can't be real (right?), but it's still super cool. How did you make the picture move like that? If it were a gif I'd understand, but it's a plain old jpg. I checked!

Stanley clicked back to his chat with Jaxon.

> STANTHEMAN64: What do they mean
> move?!?!?!
>
> DARBYFAN#1: You got me. All I see is the same
> old picture.

Stanley scrolled back up so the picture filled the screen. A skeleton torso with its back to him, the blade peeking through the grass in the bottom corner. He could understand why some people would think it was fake. If he didn't know better, he might say it was a super-realistic Halloween decoration, the kind Jaxon's dad put in his haunted house.

As he stared harder, though, a tunnel started to form around his head, the way it always does if you focus on something long enough. The image began to wobble and go blurry. All of the sounds around him – the ticking clock, the buzz of his computer fan – meshed into static that tickled the inside of his ears. It was just him and the photograph. The skull, blanched extra white in the scant moonlight. The ribs, curving in like teeth. The vertebrae, poking out like miniature sea monsters stripped of their skin.

Skull, ribs, vertebrae, shadow. The images whirred in his head, flipping over and over like one of those old-timey film reels. He might have sat there and stared at it forever, in some weird trance, except just then the impossible happened. *Skeletus animatus* moved.

His skull twisted around, so slow Stanley could hear each vertebrae crack, and he winked.

Stanley jumped back and fell out of his chair. He knocked his head on his official *Skatepark Zombie Death Bash* bite-proof helmet. A message pinged on his computer, but he was too dizzy to get up and check it.

'Sweetie, what on earth happened?'

Mom leaned over him, and he sat up so fast they nearly conked heads.

'Nothing, it's nothing, I'm fine!' He lunged for the computer, but he was moving so quickly all the blood rushed to his brain, and he ended up face-planting in the carpet.

Mom helped him up and cradled his head, but then the computer pinged with another message and her brow creased. 'You know you're not supposed to be online this late, it's already past your bedtime.' She squinted at the screen. 'What kind of website are you looking at anyway?'

Inside, a tiny part of Stanley died. His secret was out. Mom would make him take the picture off the site, and his chances of winning would be – 'Hey, where did it go?'

'What do you mean?' Mom said.

The photograph was gone. In its place was a grey square cracked down the middle, the type of thing that came up when the image that was supposed to go there was corrupted.

'It was there just a second ago. It—'

Mom shook her head and switched off the computer. 'Come on, let's go to the kitchen and I'll get you some ice for your head. This is why I don't want you staying up all hours playing games on that computer.'

'It wasn't a game,' Stanley said, and then he wished he hadn't.

'Whatever it was, I don't want you on there again tonight. You go straight to sleep, you hear me?'

'OK.'

'OK, what?'

'OK with whipped cream on top.'

'That's better.'

A few minutes later, Stanley crawled into bed, an ice

pack pricking the back of his head. He stared at his darkened computer screen. Had the picture really winked at him? Was the file actually corrupted? His fingers itched to turn on the computer and find out, but he could hear Mom puttering around in the kitchen. She was probably waiting up to make sure he went to sleep. He thought about putting a blanket under the door so she wouldn't see the light from the computer screen, but in the end it didn't matter. He fell into a deep sleep without even meaning to, a sleep full of skull and rib and shadow.

CHAPTER FOURTEEN

The next day at school, Stanley collided with Jaxon outside his locker.

'Did you see it?' they both said at the same time.

For a second, Stanley thought that Jaxon had seen the picture move, too, but then Jaxon said, 'It's gone! The file's corrupted.'

'Maybe the website's just having a glitch,' Stanley said, hopeful.

'I don't think so. It didn't affect any of the other entries.'

'Let's pull it up on the school computers to make sure.'

They hurried to the library with only five minutes before the bell rang. *Skeletus animatus* was still the number one entry, but the picture was gone. Stanley scanned through the latest comments.

YETIFINDER33: Knew it was too good to be true!

ARCHEO_NUT: Guess the admins finally figured out this was a hoax. About time!

BONEGUY2007: Cheater!

It went on and on like that. Sweat beaded on the back of Stanley's neck. 'But yesterday, everybody loved it. I don't understand.'

'They think the people running the contest took the photo down,' said Jaxon, patting Stanley's shoulder. 'We'll just have to take a better one and prove them wrong.'

'With what camera?'

'Oh, right . . . Hang on, doesn't your mom still have that camera with the fancy lens? I remember her taking photos of Miren at her kindergarten graduation.'

'That was Dad's.'

'Oh.' Jaxon looked away, like he was afraid to meet Stanley's eyes.

'What about you? Your parents must have a camera.'

'No way. Dad gave them all to charity last year when

he went through his whole Zen housecleaning phase. He said why keep all the cameras lying around when his phone could do the same thing.'

Stanley's eyes turned to Jaxon.

'Oh no, not gonna happen.'

'I didn't even say anything yet,' said Stanley.

'Yeah, well, don't bother. There's no chance Dad will let me borrow it. Trust me, I've tried. "Once you can afford to pay the bill yourself, then you can get a phone," that's what he always says. That phone is his baby. He only let me touch it once, and I had to be seated on the couch with a pillow on my lap, just in case I dropped it.'

'I never said he had to know about it,' said Stanley. No way was he going to get this far only to let the contest slip away.

Jaxon's eyes widened. Just then, the bell rang, and Jaxon nearly jumped out of his chair. 'Forget about it, Stanley.'

'He'll never find out.'

'I know you want to win, but we're talking larceny.'

'Boys, time to get to class!'

'Yes, Mrs Reed,' said Jaxon and Stanley together.

'Come on, just think about it,' Stanley said as they hurried for homeroom.

'I did think about it, and no. I'm too young to be grounded for life.'

'We won't get caught.'

'"Integrity is what you do when nobody is looking." James Darby, in Darby Brothers' Mystery #23, *The Tattle-Tale Heart*.'

They stopped outside the classroom door as the second bell rang.

'Besides,' said Jaxon, 'what would your dad say if he knew you'd won the contest by stealing?'

That question felt like a cold fork slipped into Stanley's chest. His dad hated stealing. He worked at a law firm where all they did was defend people who'd had their money stolen by big corporations.

'Boys, the classroom's in here. Would you two care to grace us with your presence?'

Stanley sighed, like he was a balloon and someone had let out all the air. He took a seat next to Jaxon, barely remembering to stand when the Pledge of Allegiance came over the loudspeaker. When they sat down again, Stanley had to try hard to keep his head from drooping on to his desk. Things were that hopeless.

He might have slumped on to the floor, right there in front of everyone, but Jaxon passed him a note when the teacher wasn't looking.

'Don't worry. We'll think of something.'

——

After school, Stanley wanted to go straight home to make more charts about the skeleton's growth, but Mom insisted he help her shop for Miren's birthday present. Her birthday was on Saturday, right before Jaxon's Halloween party, and everyone was coming. Uncle Morris was even flying in from Florida.

'Will Dad be there?' Stanley looked at the Lego on the shelf, like maybe he didn't care about the answer.

'He tried, but all the flights were booked.' Mom scratched the back of Stanley's neck with her plastic nails. Stanley shrugged out of reach and swallowed the dust bunny that had formed in his throat. Figures, he hadn't really thought Dad would be coming home anyway. He'd already missed New Year's, Fourth of July, and Stanley's birthday. He'd Skyped in for last Christmas, but that didn't count.

'Look, Stanley, they have Princess Mayflower Pony. She sailed the seas with Christopher Columbus, and she sparkles,' Mom read off the side of the package, probably trying to cheer him up.

They put the pony and a pack of pink-and-purple Lego in the cart. Mom let Stanley pick out the gift bag and party favours. He chose jiggly rubber skeletons and kazoos that hiccupped when you blew on them.

'Are you sure she'll like those?' Mom said.

Stanley was sure.

At the checkout, the little screen flashed DECLINED after Mom swiped her credit card. That had only happened once when Dad was home, and that had been a mistake. Now it happened all the time.

'Sorry, you'll have to try another one,' said the clerk.

'Hold on.' Mom's cheeks flushed. The people behind them moved to another line. Stanley felt the skin on the back of his ears grow hot. 'Can you take off the Lego, and the kazoos? Sorry, Stanley.'

'It's OK,' Stanley said. What else could he say? He knew how embarrassed she got whenever stuff like this happened, and it wasn't her fault. She did the best she could, only keeping a whole family together wasn't supposed to be a one-person job.

'Swipe your card again.'

The screen flashed ACCEPTED.

'Good to go,' said the clerk. 'Would you like

your receipt in the bag?'

In the car park, Mom stowed the bags in the boot. She waited for Stanley to climb into the passenger seat, and then she closed the door behind him. He watched in the rearview mirror as she shut her eyes and ran a hand over her face. She stood like that for a while before she climbed into the car and started the engine.

On the way home, Mom's phone buzzed in her bag.

'Can you get it?' Mom said. It had started to rain again, and she was straining to see through the smeared windshield.

'Sure.' Stanley flipped open the phone. 'Hello?'

'Oh, it's the little one. Tell Momma to come to Spring Hill Clinic. Use the emergency entrance. Tell her now, Stanley.' Ms Francine's voice shook in his ears.

Stanley told Mom.

'What do you mean the emergency entrance?'

'She says to go now,' Stanley said. His fingers gripped the phone so tight they went numb. 'She'll meet us outside. Hurry, Mom.'

CHAPTER FIFTEEN

Mom held Stanley's hand as they ran up to the emergency entrance. She left her bag and keys in the car.

'I'll get them later, Stanley. We have to find your sister.' She sounded angry, but Stanley didn't think she was angry at him.

'Oh god, where is she?' Mom collapsed into Ms Francine's arms.

Ms Francine used her stiff shoulders to keep Mom from falling. 'She's OK. Come inside and I'll show you.' She crooked a finger at Stanley. 'You, too. Follow Ms Francine.'

She led them past a waiting room full of screaming, red-faced babies. One boy about Stanley's age sat in a wheelchair, both legs wrapped in heavy casts.

'I don't understand why this happened,' Mom said, her voice muffled by Ms Francine's woolly sweater. 'She was doing so well. She hasn't even used her oxygen tank since . . .' Mom stopped dead in the hallway. 'Oh my god, the oxygen tank.'

'It's not your fault, Momma.' Mom started to slip and Ms Francine held her tighter. 'The little one is fine. The doctor said she can pick a treasure from his chest, whatever this means. Next time, you'll remember.'

Stanley didn't understand what they were talking about. Then they went to Miren's room, and Stanley saw the tubes hooked up to her nose and the machine that went whoosh, whoosh when it breathed for her. The oxygen tank. It had been in Mom's boot the whole time. He remembered it clanking around back there when they drove to the toy store.

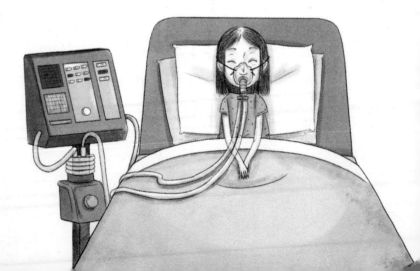

'Stanley!' Miren pulled the plastic mask from her face and tried to climb out of bed.

'Don't move, sweetheart.' Mom tucked Miren back in and kneeled at her side. 'I'm so sorry.' She said something else, but the words got all choked up in her throat.

'It's OK, Momma.' A concerned look pinched Miren's forehead, and she patted Mom's shoulder the same way Ms Francine had.

Mom started to laugh and cry at the same time.

Stanley came around to the other side of the bed and examined Miren's treasures. Three this time. A Koosh ball, a plastic harmonica, and one of those army guys with a parachute on his back.

'That one's for you,' Miren said.

Stanley hugged her. She smelt like sweat and laundry soap. 'How do you feel, Mir-Bear?'

'Guess what?' Miren said as Mom stroked her hair.

'What?'

'Skeleton-Butt!' Miren heaved with laughter. The laugh turned into a cough, and Mom fastened the mask back over Miren's mouth.

'Just for a little while, sweetheart. Breathe in.'

'Who's thirsty?' Ms Francine said, standing in the

doorway. 'I get everyone a drink. And a Butterfinger for Stanley. Momma, what can I get you?'

'Nothing, thank you.' She bit her lower lip. 'I'm so sorry this happened.'

'No time for sorry. This is what we say in Kyrgyzstan. Only time to shear the sheep, and maybe milk the cows.' She swatted a hand at Mom. 'I get you a Mars bar, good?' She left without waiting for an answer.

The doctor came in and gave Miren some medicine that dripped from a tube into her wrist and made her fall asleep. He said they wanted to observe Miren overnight, and then he left to find a camp bed for Mom.

'You go home with Ms Francine,' Mom said. 'I'll order you a taxi.' Ms Francine had never learned to drive.

'I'm staying with Miren.' Stanley was tired of Mom treating him like a little kid. He took care of Miren at home; he could do it here, too.

Mom sighed. 'You sleep on the camp bed, then. I'll take the chair.'

'No, Mom. I'm fine.' He curled up in the chair to show her it was a perfect fit.

'Sweets and drinks.' Ms Francine handed out the snacks and left Miren's on the table by her bed. 'And you might be wanting this.' She set Mom's keys and bag on the counter next to the sink.

'How did you know I'd left them?' Mom said, getting up to hug Ms Francine.

'I know.' Ms Francine tapped the side of her nose the way she always did.

They played Crazy Eights on a rolling tray table, and then Mom called a taxi for Ms Francine around midnight.

'I come back first thing in the morning. Call me if you need me sooner.'

'What would we do without you, Belka?'

Stanley must have looked confused, because Ms Francine said, 'Belka Francine Bolotova. What can I say? This is my name.'

Stanley squeezed Ms Francine's bony hips. A tiny voice murmured something, and they all turned around to see Miren sit up in bed.

'What was that, sweetie?' Mom said.

'Skeleton-Butt,' Ms Francine whispered in Stanley's ear. 'They grow so fast.' She shook her head, and Stanley watched her fuzzy sweater disappear down the hall, under the sputtering incandescent lights.

CHAPTER SIXTEEN

Mom made Stanley go to school the next day, while she stayed home from work and took care of Miren. Stanley didn't listen when Mr. Crouch told him to take his head off the desk and pay attention. He ignored the nurse when she asked him to open up and say 'aah.'

'I can't believe you didn't get detention,' Jaxon said. He fed a coin into the vending machine. 'You should have called me last night, by the way, and told me you were at the hospital. I messaged you seventeen times.'

Stanley shrugged, but he couldn't bring himself to

answer. If he did, he'd have to tell Jaxon how scared he'd been seeing Miren in that hospital bed.

'Oh well, no big deal. I hope it wasn't anything serious.'

Suddenly, Stanley felt a burning need to change the subject. 'Hey, do you want to come to my house after school? We should get started on those charts, and then we can look for your iPad some more in the garden. We have to find it, it's our only chance.'

'Yeah, sure.' Jaxon paused and bit his lower lip. Once, twice, three times. 'Stanley, you know how some people in the comments sections said they saw the picture move, I mean before it disappeared? Well, it's just, right before it went away I was looking at it and I could have sworn I saw . . .'

'Skeleton-Butt?' Stanley said.

'What?' Juice squirted out of Jaxon's nose, but he looked relieved not to have to finish.

'My sentiments exactly.'

After a long and farty bus ride, Stanley and Jaxon raced into the kitchen to find Miren colouring at the kitchen table. She had the tubes stuffed up her nose again and chocolate smeared across her cheeks.

'Stanley! Ms Francine made cookies, and I ate so many I have a food baby. See?'

Miren stuck out her stomach and rubbed it like she was pregnant.

'Gross.'

'You're gross.' She squirmed out of the chair, but Stanley caught her before she could pull the tubes loose.

'This one has the energy of a steam engine. You watch out for her.' Ms Francine shook her head and put a second plate of cookies on the table. 'Peanut butter chocolate chip. What can I say, I try something different. Sorry, Stanley, this batch is not from a tube.'

'Where's Mom?' Stanley said.

'Momma had to work the night shift. She said she was sorry she didn't get to see you before she left. Eat a cookie before they get cold.'

Stanley picked up one of the cookies. It was so soft the chocolate oozed between his fingers. 'That's OK,' he said, mouth full of gooey sweetness. 'Hey, these are pretty good.'

After his fifth cookie, Ms Francine shooed them all out of the kitchen with a dish towel. 'Go outside and check on your tree. Some of us have dinner to cook. And make sure that little one wears a jacket.'

'It's not a tree,' Jaxon said, but Stanley knew it was no use arguing with Ms Francine.

Stanley zipped Miren into her favourite Stripy Pony jacket, and they all went outside to look at the thing that was not a tree. For once, he wasn't annoyed at having Miren along. Jaxon took a sketch pad and a measuring tape from his coat pocket and started to take notes.

'The arms do kind of look like branches,' Stanley said, tilting his head up at the skeleton. Bony arms stretched towards the sky, skull bent back. Like he was waiting for it to rain.

'I can almost see his ankles,' Jaxon said, shaking his head and counting the fence slats under his breath while he drew.

As he said it, the bones scooted out of the earth another inch. Jaxon squeezed his pencil so hard the lead broke. Stanley gasped and Miren clapped her hands by his ear. Stanley pulled her into his lap to keep her from racing around and knocking over the tank. Which was pretty painful, since she was almost eight and, ironically, had a super-bony butt.

'You know, I guess it is like a tree,' Jaxon said after a long silence. His voice sounded like he'd just finished running a ten-mile race. 'The Darby Brothers would never believe you have a skeleton growing in your garden, Stanley, and I don't think I do, either. And I'm looking right at it.'

'The Darby Brothers aren't real,' Stanley said.

Jaxon didn't say anything for a while, and then he tossed his notebook aside and shoved a peanut butter cookie in his mouth. 'I give up. No matter how many notes I take, no one is ever going to believe this.' He shook his head, like he was responding to a question no one had asked. 'I wonder why it's here. I mean, skeletons don't just show up and—'

Miren coughed a piece of cookie on to her shoe. She clutched her chest and kept coughing until a string of yellow spittle dribbled out of her mouth. Stanley wiped it away. He didn't gag, not even a little, but Miren still started to cry. The tears came in great waves that shook her entire body.

'Should I go get Ms Francine?' Jaxon said.

'I can handle it,' said Stanley. He patted her shoulder and pushed back her hair. He even did the Donald Duck voice that always made her laugh. Nothing worked.

'Maybe I should go get Ms Francine. Just in case.'

'No, I got it.' Stanley had always been the only one who could cheer Miren up when she felt sick.

Something click-clacked behind him. He turned around to see two gaping black eye sockets staring down at him. The skeleton held up a finger, like it had just got an idea. Then it started to dance.

It moved slowly at first, swaying its bottom and waving its arms. Then it knocked its knees together and bobbed its head. Music tinkled in Stanley's ears, but he couldn't tell where it was coming from.

Miren wiped the tears from her face and her mouth dropped open. She watched the skeleton twirl his arms and slap out a beat on his thigh bones. Her face split into a grin when he stuck out his bottom and bopped it up and down to the mysterious beat.

'Come on, Stanley,' she said, some of her energy returning. 'Time to dance!'

Stanley didn't know what to do. Maybe Jaxon was right. A skeleton couldn't grow in a garden, and it definitely couldn't dance. But here it was, doing both things at once. Maybe he was hallucinating, like those guys in the movies who see lush rivers in the middle of the desert, only to find out they're not really there.

'Dance, Bony-Butt, come on. Please!'

Arms numb, Stanley helped Miren up, and they kind of rocked side to side. It wasn't exactly dancing, but it was the best he could do with the tubes tying her down to her tank.

'Oh, here.' Jaxon sighed, like he couldn't believe what he was about to do. He picked up her tank, so that Miren could move more freely.

And that was how it happened. Stanley, Jaxon, and Miren, all dancing together with a skeleton that probably didn't exist. They danced until the tears dried on Miren's cheeks and Stanley's arms burned from holding so much of her weight.

When his arms turned to jelly and he couldn't hold her up one more second, Stanley set Miren down, and she fell back on the grass, giggling. The tinkling music faded away, and the skeleton went still. Stanley and Jaxon sank on to the grass, too, only they weren't giggling. They were staring at each other, one more perplexed than the other.

The two boys sat like that in stillness, listening to

Miren go on about how much fun she had dancing with Princy, until Jaxon's mom finally came to pick him up.

'Bye,' Jaxon managed. He chewed his lower lip. 'Stanley, maybe it's time you told someone about the skeleton. You know, a real grown-up, not Ms Francine.'

Stanley didn't answer. What could he say? Jaxon knew his mom couldn't see the skeleton, and he doubted any other grown-ups could, either. Which meant there was no point in telling, and probably – his heart sank – no hope for winning the contest. Even if he could upload another shot, who would believe him? The people online already thought the whole thing was a hoax.

'Come inside, little ones,' Ms Francine called after Jaxon had left. 'Time to eat tea. And surprise, I ordered pizza for dinner. It's no borscht, but what can I do?'

They ate pizza and more cookies. Even though it was delicious, Stanley had a hard time swallowing. Ms Francine told them stories about her goat, Bakyt, and how they'd taught him to juggle one summer to make extra money. For once, Stanley was happy to listen to her. It meant he didn't have to talk or think about what had just happened.

After he'd helped Ms Francine rinse the dishes, he went to tuck Miren into bed.

'Sweet dreams, Mir-Bear.' He kissed her forehead. It tasted like grass and cookies.

'Stanley,' Miren said. 'I want to see Princy dance at my birthday party. By then I'll feel better and I won't have my stupid tank and I can really dance.'

'His name isn't Princy,' Stanley said.

'But can he dance at my party? I want Ashleigh to see him, and Stripy Pony, and maybe Uncle Morris. Also my friends from school. They'll be so surprised their heads will probably fall off.'

Stanley hadn't considered what would happen on Saturday, when everybody came over to the house for Miren's party. A bubble of greasy pepperoni pizza gurgled up the back of his throat.

'I don't know, Mir-Bear. We'll have to see.'

'OK, 'night Stanley.'

He turned out the lights and padded to the back window. The skeleton glowed in the pale moonlight. Inside, a metal clamp pinched Stanley's stomach, and it wasn't just about the contest. He couldn't explain why, but a tiny part of him didn't want anyone else to know about the skeleton, not any more. If Uncle Morris and everybody saw it, that would mean it was real . . . really real . . . and everything that had happened since the skeleton had started to grow was real, too. Like the oxygen tank and Miren going to the hospital.

He blinked, and dark clouds passed overhead, hiding the skeleton from view. No, he was being stupid. The skeleton didn't have anything to do with Miren getting sick; how could it? Besides, if he won the contest, there was a chance Dad would decide to come home, and that was what Miren really needed. She'd never been this sick when Dad was here. Mom tried her best, but without Dad the three of them were like a hot air balloon without a pilot. Floating higher and higher into the clouds until the balloon came apart and they were just scraps of old fabric drifting on the wind.

CHAPTER SEVENTEEN

On Saturday morning, the day of Miren's party, Ms Francine baked lemon cupcakes while Stanley blew up balloons. Stanley and Jaxon had spent the whole week thinking of another way to get a camera, but so far they hadn't come up with one. Jaxon had even used his allowance money to buy an old-school disposable camera, but when they got the pictures developed the next day, all they'd captured were blurry white streaks.

The situation was desperate. Today was the last day to edit entries. The night before, Jaxon had uploaded some of his charts and sketches, but they weren't as good as a photograph. They'd fallen to number three in the rankings, behind some kid in Indiana who'd discovered an ancient arthropod fossil and a girl in Idaho who claimed to have uncovered a foot-long piece of dinosaur poo.

'Why so many worry lines, little Stanley? Everything will be ready by party time,' said Ms Francine, sneaking up on him. 'Boys nowadays. If you aren't careful, you'll look like an old man by the time you're twenty.'

Stanley shook his head and blew hard into a pink balloon. Ms Francine didn't know anything. The party was the least of his worries.

Miren was spending the day at a friend's house so she wouldn't see the decorations before the party. Jaxon came over after breakfast and helped Stanley hang yellow streamers and place rubber skeletons all over the polka-dot tablecloth.

'Don't talk to me, then.' Ms Francine swatted a hand at him. 'Who needs you when I have my cupcakes to talk to.'

When she was gone, Jaxon leaned in. 'How's Princy today?'

Stanley threw a skeleton at Jaxon's face. It slapped the side of his nose and stuck there.

'Hey, what was that for?'

'His name isn't Princy,' Stanley said, not bothering to keep his voice down. What was the point? Ms Francine already knew everything.

'Then what is it?'

'He doesn't have one.'

They hung the Stripy Pony piñata in front of the fireplace and set out Miren's presents on the hall table.

'What'd you get her?' Stanley said, eying the pink-and-purple bag Jaxon pulled from his backpack.

'The complete beginner's set of Darby Brothers' mysteries, numbers one to five.'

'She'll love it,' Stanley said.

'I know what sarcasm is, Stanley, I'm not stupid. Anyway, I also got her a model skeleton. The plastic kind with squishy organs inside.'

Stanley wished he'd thought of that. 'Hey, do you smell something?'

Stanley and Jaxon peeked into the kitchen just as Ms Francine was frosting a batch of puffy lemon cupcakes.

'No fingers!' she shouted, but it was too late. Stanley had already swiped a gob of frosting from the top of the nearest cupcake. She shooed them outside with her spatula, and both boys fell on the grass, laughing.

'Wow, she's serious about her cupcakes,' Jaxon said.

'In Kyrgyzstan, you can probably buy eleven goats for a single cupcake.'

'Doubtful, I'm pretty sure the economic situation there is pretty similar to – oh, right, sarcasm.'

Stanley stood up and dusted off his jeans. 'Hey, check out the skeleton formerly known as Princy.'

'What?'

'Never mind, just come over here. He's out of the ground.' Stanley ran up to the foot of the skeleton. 'I can even see his toes.'

'He looks like he's going somewhere,' Jaxon said. 'Or getting ready to run a marathon.'

Jaxon was right; the skeleton seemed to have frozen mid-stride. 'He reminds me of one of those explorer guys, setting off on some big adventure.' Stanley had seen a picture of a famous explorer once, venturing across the arctic steppe. He'd had the same expression on his face, fear and wonder and anticipation all mixed into one.

'Yeah, I guess. Ooh, do you think we can make him dance again?' Jaxon said. He didn't look so scared any more after their impromptu dance party.

'I don't know.' Stanley tapped carefully on one of his ribs. It sent vibrations down the entire skeleton that reverberated in Stanley's finger. 'Maybe he doesn't like to be ordered around.'

'That makes sense,' Jaxon said. Now Jaxon was the one being sarcastic.

They stood back and stared at the thing that had grown from a tiny finger into a full-fledged skeleton in a matter of days. Looking at it made the breath get all thick and sticky in Stanley's throat. This was what he'd wanted, for the skeleton to come out of the ground so he could use it to win the contest. But discoveries weren't supposed to happen this way. Bones didn't dig themselves up, at least not normal ones.

Ms Francine kept calling it a tree, and maybe that made some kind of sense, but it didn't look like that to Stanley. Trees were natural. They didn't carry around creepy blades or wear black hoods or wink at people in photographs.

And skeletons were supposed to stay underground, buried, where they belonged.

'You know what this means, don't you?' said Jaxon. His expression had changed from one of fear, when he'd looked at the skeleton before, to one of admiration. 'We have to find a way to get a picture now that we can see the whole specimen.'

'He's not a specimen,' Stanley said. 'And the deadline is midnight tonight. It's hopeless.' Stanley never thought those words would come out of his mouth, but now that he'd said them, they lodged like rocks in the back of his throat and made it impossible to swallow.

'Then what is he? If he's not a specimen?' said Jaxon.

Stanley shrugged; Jaxon was missing the point. 'I don't know, all I'm saying is specimens don't dance.'

Stanley stood on his tiptoes and peered into the skeleton's eye sockets. He looked down and down, and could have looked down some more, except a shiver crackled up his spine and into his palms, and he decided it wouldn't do any good to look more closely. He'd made the greatest discovery of anyone in the contest – he was sure of it – but now no one would ever know.

'Excuse me, is this the Stanwright residence? I'm here to deliver . . . whoa.'

Stanley spun around to see a boy in a bright blue uniform gaping at him through the back door.

The boy went all fish-eyed and stumbled into the doorframe. 'What the – I mean, dude, is that a real skeleton?'

'Um . . .' said Stanley.

'Well, the thing is . . .' Jaxon explained.

'What should we do?' Stanley whispered in Jaxon's ear, a hummingbird pounding out a beat inside his chest.

'OK, let me think . . . If we were James and Oliver Darby, how would we . . .'

'Hey, can I touch it?' The pizza boy had started across the lawn when a booming voice stopped him.

'There you are, Mr Pizza Man. I see you met Hector, our model skeleton.' Ms Francine stomped over and stood in the pizza boy's path. 'A prop, you know, like from the movies. For the little girl's party. It is Halloween, after all.' Stanley nodded vigorously. Ms Francine folded some bills into the boy's hands, but he never took his eyes off the skeleton. 'Here you go, and keep the change.'

The boy still didn't move, so Ms Francine swatted his shoulder. 'Go on already. Are you a pizza delivery boy or a statue? Get, get!'

Stanley couldn't help laughing at the sight of Ms Francine chasing the pizza boy out of the house with her spatula. But he was also worried.

'Do you think he'll tell anyone?'

'About Princy? No way. Who would believe him?'

'Yeah, I guess that makes sense.' Just like the people online who'd said his discovery was a hoax.

Ms Francine clucked her tongue at them when she came back outside. 'I hope you two have plans for him . . .' She waved a hand at the skeleton. '. . . for today, I mean. You can't parade him about like he's a carnival sideshow. You need to think creatively.' She slammed the door and went back to frosting her cupcakes.

'She's right,' Stanley said. 'He might look like a Halloween decoration, but what if he moves? And what if people start asking questions? You know how good Miren is at keeping secrets.'

'But she's not – oh, right.'

'Exactly. We have to cover him up, at least until after the party. But how?'

Jaxon sketched out some ideas, and finally they came up with the perfect way to disguise the skeleton. The metal clamp in Stanley's stomach loosened, just a little. If they could hide him until everyone went home, then find a way to get a new picture, they still had a chance at the contest.

'What if he doesn't like being covered up?' Jaxon said as he twirled yellow streamers around the skull.

'He was underground until a few days ago,' said Stanley. 'I don't think he'll mind.'

'Oh yeah, you're probably right.'

Once the skeleton was wound up like a lemon-flavoured mummy, Stanley and Jaxon went into the garage to cut out a huge cardboard circle. Jaxon painted it orange, red, and green.

'There.' Stanley taped the circle to the top of the skeleton. 'Now he looks like a giant lollipop. Nobody will ever know the difference.'

'And if he moves?' Jaxon said.

'We'll just say it's the wind. That should work. Right?'

Both boys spun around as the doorbell rang.

'I sure hope so,' Jaxon said. 'Because we just ran out of time.'

Uncle Morris trundled in carrying a package so big he had to go through the door sideways.

'Stan the Man! How goes it? And Jaxon with an *x*, right? Funny name. Hey, help me get this package on the table.' Uncle Morris's cheeks had gone red above his bristly beard.

'I don't think it'll fit, Uncle Morris,' Stanley said. The package was bigger than the table. 'Maybe you should put it in the living room.'

'What's in there anyway?' Jaxon said.

Uncle Morris heaved the package on to the carpet

and collapsed into an armchair. As he did, something thin and silver fell out of his pocket and caught between the chair cushions. Stanley's eyes met Jaxon's. It was a phone – he was sure of it.

'I could tell you,' he said in his best arch-villain voice, 'but then I'd have to kill you!'

'Nobody says that any more.' Stanley looked at Jaxon, who nodded. In his mind, he was already thinking of ways to make Uncle Morris move so he could get to the phone.

'No? Oh well.' He threw up his hands. 'Then I guess I'll tell you, but no blabbing. Got it?'

'Got it,' Stanley said.

'OK, it's an official Stripy Pony mini motorized convertible, complete with tail brush.'

'Tail brush?' Jaxon said.

'Yeah, it has this tail thing coming out of the boot. Don't ask me. Point is, you can brush it. Hey . . .' Uncle Morris sniffed the air like a lion scenting prey. '. . . who ordered pizza?'

'I might have ordered it,' said Ms Francine. 'Hard to tell.' She shook hands with Uncle Morris. 'Now, who wants to come into the kitchen and help me with the candles?'

'I do,' Uncle Morris said, standing up with a groan. 'Oh, you mean the kiddos?'

'No, no,' said Ms Francine. 'The big kiddo will do just fine.'

Uncle Morris went into the kitchen to help Ms Francine. Stanley looked at Jaxon. Jaxon shook his head, but it was already too late. Stanley sat down in the chair, and with his back to the kitchen slid the phone into his pocket.

'What are you doing?' Jaxon whispered, eyes wide. 'That doesn't belong to you. Why don't you just ask to borrow it?'

'We'll go out and snap a shot while he's distracted, and then we'll put it back where we found it.'

'Where *you* found it. And besides, the skeleton's all wrapped up, remember?'

Stanley hadn't thought about that. 'We'll just have to hurry.'

'There's no time. The party will start any minute now.'

'No way, we've got at least—'

The doorbell rang again.

Stanley let his head thump into the back of the puffy leather chair. 'I'll get it,' he called, keeping his hand over the pocket where he was hiding the phone.

He opened the door to find a woman in a blue police uniform. His heart stopped for a full second before it started up again at a frantic pace.

'Oh . . . my . . . god,' Jaxon said, coming up behind Stanley. 'Please tell me this is a costume party.'

'It's not.'

'Oh.'

A million things ran through Stanley's head in that moment. First and foremost, that somehow someone knew he'd stolen the phone and he was about to get arrested. The phone, which before had felt cool to the touch, burned against his skin.

'Sorry to bother you,' she said. 'I'm Officer Knokes. Is your mom or dad home?'

'No, she's out. Can I . . . help you?' Stanley said, trying hard to keep from hyperventilating.

Officer Knokes adjusted her belt. 'I'd rather speak with the head of the household. Is there an adult at home?'

'What can I do for you, Ms Policewoman?' Ms Francine said, sneaking up behind Stanley and Jaxon. 'I hope we haven't broken any laws? Unless it's a crime now to have a party?'

Stanley tightened his grip on the phone in his pocket. Officer Knokes swept her gaze over his trousers and then took in the presents and decorations. 'Listen, I'm sorry to intrude, folks, I'm sure it's a misunderstanding, but we've received a tip that you might be keeping a dead body on the premises.'

'A dead what?' Uncle Morris stumbled out of the kitchen, holding a lit birthday candle. For a moment, relief flooded Stanley's chest; that is, until he realized what must have happened.

'Like I said, I'm sure it's a mistake, but if I could just take a quick look around—'

'And who exactly made this tip?' Ms Francine raised an eyebrow. 'It wouldn't be a certain pizza boy who was fifteen minutes late making his delivery?'

'I can't divulge that information, ma'am. If you could just show me your garden, I'll be on my way.'

Every eye turned to the back window. Stanley's breath caught in his throat. In the spot where he should have seen a giant paper lollipop, he found nothing but air. Ms Francine winked at him and tapped the side of her nose. He looked at Jaxon, whose eyebrows reached all the way up to the top of his hair.

'OK, we will show you. Hurry up, Ms Policewoman,

it's almost party time, and we wouldn't want to ruin a little girl's birthday.'

'Of course not, ma'am.'

Ms Francine showed Officer Knokes around the garden. Stanley and Jaxon went outside, too, and stared down at the spot where the skeleton had been.

'What do you think happened to him?' Jaxon whispered, his breath coming in short gasps. 'I mean, skeletons don't get up and walk away. Do they?'

'This one might.' Stanley nodded to the fence, where a bit of yellow streamer had caught in between two slats. It swished back and forth in the wind, creating an eerie sort of music. Stanley hugged his arms tight around his chest. He couldn't explain it, but he had the strangest feeling, like the streamer was inside his rib cage, tickling his bones.

CHAPTER EIGHTEEN

Officer Knokes apologized to Ms Francine and climbed back into her patrol car. While everyone was in the hallway, showing her out, Stanley slipped the phone back in between the chair cushions. What was the point in having a camera if there wasn't anything to take a picture of? His heart sank a little deeper in his chest.

'Most of these tips turn out to be false alarms,' she said over the crackle of the scanner. 'Especially on Halloween.'

'It's OK, we understand. These birthday parties can be dangerous things. Goodbye, now,' Ms Francine said. She waved a clawed hand at Officer Knokes and led Jaxon and Uncle Morris back inside.

'What was that all about?' said Uncle Morris. 'I don't come to visit for six months, and now you're hiding dead bodies on the premises?'

'We're not hiding dead bodies. It was just a mistake,'

Stanley said, the words tasting hollow in his mouth. 'You heard her, they get false alarms all the time.'

'All right, I trust you. But if you're planning to break the law again, warn me next time, OK? I've got priors.'

'No, you don't.'

'Oh, a smart alec and a criminal? Mom is gonna love this.'

'You're not gonna tell her,' Stanley said, almost cracking a smile.

In response, Uncle Morris released the wettest, smelliest burp Stanley had ever witnessed.

'Probably not.' Uncle Morris winked. 'Your secret life of crime is safe with me. Now, you and your sidekick over there . . .' He pointed to Jaxon. '. . . come and help me hang these lights in the garden.'

'But it's still daytime,' said Jaxon.

'For later, duh. Don't make me burp on you again.'

'We'd better help him.' Jaxon looked at Uncle Morris's mouth like it was a rubbish bin on the verge of exploding. 'I think he means business.'

By the time Miren's friends from school started to show up at the door with gift bags as big as they were, grey clouds had blocked out the sun. Uncle Morris was right about the lights. They sparkled, warm and inviting, making Stanley almost glad for the grey, stormy sky. They reminded him of the glow-in-the-dark pony set Dad had given Miren for her last birthday. Too bad Dad wouldn't be giving Miren anything like that this year, at least not in person.

While they waited for Mom and the birthday girl, Ms Francine entertained the guests in the living room with stories of life in Kyrgyzstan.

'Every morning, I woke up at five to get water from the well. Two miles I had to walk, and when it was snowing, the well would be one big sheet of ice. If I was lucky, I would make it back home without breaking my neck. Then it was time to peel potatoes.'

Stanley retreated to the garden. He closed his eyes and tried to remember what it was like this time last year when Dad still lived with them. He couldn't. It seemed so long ago.

'I found those cut-outs you were looking for,' Jaxon said to Uncle Morris. 'The ones of Stripy Pony. We could still put them up.'

'Way to go, Jaxon with an *x*. You're turning out to be quite the treasure hunter. Help me stick 'em on the fence, would you? Wherever you can find space.'

'Or,' Jaxon said, 'we could make it look like they're running.'

Uncle Morris rubbed his chin. 'I like how this kid thinks. Let's do it, quick, before Miren gets here.'

They taped Uncle Morris's glittery pony cut-outs along the fence so it looked like the horses were running. Underneath the sparkly lights, they really did look pretty awesome. Stanley hated ponies, but he knew Miren would love them. Even though, for some reason, seeing them made him a little sad.

'Hey, check out the fence,' Jaxon whispered, peeking over his shoulder at Uncle Morris. 'The streamer that was stuck between the slats. It's gone.' Jaxon took a bunch of deep breaths, the way pregnant ladies always do on TV right before they give birth.

'That means he's out there somewhere. Hiding.' Stanley shuddered, though part of him wasn't surprised. Part of him knew, when he saw the skeleton posed like an explorer, that it was only a matter of time before . . . 'Look, I know the haunted house is tonight, but what do you say after this we go find him?'

'Find him?' Jaxon shook his head. He twirled his watch around and around his wrist, like he didn't even know he was doing it. 'You don't get it, do you?' His expression had changed back from admiration to fear. 'First, a skeleton grows in your garden. Then he gets up and walks away the minute someone discovers him. This is bad, Stanley. Horror movie bad. There's a skeleton lurking out there somewhere.' He motioned to the overgrown field beyond the fence. 'This isn't even about the contest any more. What if he sneaks into your bedroom when you're sleeping? What if he—'

The back door burst open, creaking on the broken hinge.

'Stanley! It's party time!'

Miren wiggled out of Mom's grasp. Uncle Morris caught her and spun her around in a circle, careful not to tangle her tubes.

'There you are, munchkin. Happy birthday! Give your uncle a kiss.' Uncle Morris blew a slobbery kiss into Miren's ear.

Miren giggled and squirmed as Uncle Morris set her and her tank back on the ground. Her eyes fell on the spot where the skeleton had been, and her smile crumpled. She searched the rest of the garden, and when she didn't find a skeleton, her face drooped and wobbled and threatened to explode.

'Where is he, Stanley? Where's Princy?' Her voice sounded all wispy, like someone had punched her in the stomach. 'He was supposed to dance at my party. Remember, Stanley? You promised.'

Miren ran to the spot where the skeleton had been a few minutes before, ripping out her plastic tubes and tipping over her tank.

'What did you do to him?' Miren glared at Stanley, and then, for reasons inexplicable to him, she collapsed on to the grass and started to cry. 'It's all your fault, you ruined everything.'

Uncle Morris scooped Miren up like a baby, and Mom rushed over to fix the tank. Miren sobbed and hiccupped, air rattling inside her tiny chest.

'Maybe he had to go run some errands,' Jaxon said, tugging so hard on his watch the band popped. 'I know! I bet he went to buy you a birthday present, right, Stanley?'

Stanley didn't answer. Now Mom was glaring at him, too.

'Who on earth is Princy?' Mom tried to reattach the tubes, but Miren shook her off. 'Sweetheart, you need to put them back in. Oh my god, Morris, put her down.'

Miren was choking. Uncle Morris put her down and Mom cradled her face.

'What's wrong with her, Mom?' All of a sudden, Stanley couldn't breathe, either, like a bony spider had crawled up his throat.

Mom swallowed hard but didn't answer. Miren's pudgy fingers felt cold in Stanley's hands. He tried to slide one of the tubes back in her nose, but Mom pushed him away.

'Stanley, move over. Let me do it.'

Miren's eyelids flickered.

'What's happening to her?' Stanley said, but Mom didn't answer. She secured the second tube, and Miren drew in a wheezing breath, like one of the ancient alien mummies in *Ancient Aliens Attack!* Only this wasn't some dumb video game – it was his little sister.

Stanley patted Miren's back to try to help her breathe, but Mom said, 'Scoot over, Stanley, I need to check her tank.' She fiddled with the dials. 'Tell everyone to go inside. I don't want them staring at her like this, not on her birthday.' All around them, Miren's friends and their parents turned away and headed back towards the house. 'You, too, Stanley.'

'Don't worry, sis. We'll take care of it.' Uncle Morris ushered everyone back inside, including Stanley and Jaxon, and started a sombre game of animal charades.

Stanley pressed his cheek into the cool brick fireplace, anger burning underneath his skin. Mom didn't think he could take care of Miren. She didn't know anything. He'd been the one to put a plaster on her scraped elbow the time she'd slipped on the ice. He'd taught her how to throw water balloons and ride a tricycle and eat an ice-cream cone without getting a cold headache. He never did anything *but* take care of Miren.

Mom was just too busy at her stupid job to notice. She trusted Uncle Morris, even though he only saw Miren maybe once a year, but not Stanley.

A few minutes later, Mom led Miren back inside. Everyone clapped and started to sing 'Happy Birthday', except for Stanley.

'Stanley, sing me "Happy Birthday"!' Miren pulled free of Mom's grasp and came to sit in Stanley's lap. Her butt crunched his thigh bone, but he didn't say anything. She squished his lips together to make it look like he was singing.

He wanted to stay angry, but Miren had this frustrating way of always making him laugh. He sang

'Happy Birthday', and he gave Miren a hug. Mom sat down next to him and put her arm around his shoulders. She smelt like her usual orange peel shampoo.

'You're a good big brother,' Mom said once everyone had finished singing and Ms Francine emerged from the kitchen, holding a tray of cupcakes.

'I was just trying to help,' Stanley said. Not that anyone had noticed.

'I know, I'm sorry, I've been kind of on edge lately with everything that's happening . . . You know I love you, right?'

Stanley let the words hang in the air between them. Part of him wanted to say nothing. Part of him thought Mom deserved that after always ignoring him, after refusing to trust him with Miren.

Part of him wanted to hold a grudge, but the other part knew Miren was watching. And as much as he wanted to stay angry, deep down, he also knew Mom was doing her best. It wasn't easy trying to take care of him and Miren all by herself. She might not be perfect, but she was still his mom. 'Love you, too,' he said.

'Me, too!' Miren slobbered in Stanley's ear.

'Gah!'

'Now let's eat some cupcakes,' Miren said.

She ate one bite of her cupcake, then got bored and decided to open presents.

Stanley watched and laughed at how excited she got over the dumbest things, even Jaxon's set of Darby Brothers' mysteries. He bit into his cupcake. It tasted tangy and delicious, but the sugary icing clung to the roof of his mouth. He turned to look out the window, and even though it was too cloudy to see, he couldn't shake the feeling that someone was out there, looking back at him. Waiting.

CHAPTER NINETEEN

The sun slipped out of sight as the last guest drove away. Stanley and Jaxon took down the sparkly lights and pony cut-outs, casting the garden in total darkness. The only hint of light came from the blinking Santa on Mrs Hammelstein's roof, the one she'd had up since last Christmas.

'I wonder if he's coming back.' Jaxon curled the stack of paper ponies in his hands.

Stanley didn't have to ask who he was talking about. 'There are still a few hours before midnight. If he comes back, maybe . . .' He didn't bother to finish. There was no point.

A crumpled pony dropped from the stack and landed on Jaxon's shoe. 'I hope he stays away. Sorry, Stanley, but I have a bad feeling about this . . .' He closed his eyes and shook his head, the way he always did, like he was waiting for his ears to pop. 'I just hope he stays away.'

Part of Stanley felt the same way, but the other part, the bigger part, still wished he could win the contest. When Dad was here everything felt balanced. Like how a seesaw needs someone on both sides to keep it upright. Now it was him and Mom and Miren on one side, and inch by inch they were sinking into the ground.

While Mom and Ms Francine stood on the porch, waving goodbye, Jaxon and Stanley went inside to get ready.

'I'm really sorry about the contest,' Jaxon said, strapping on his BrainBlaster 2000 chest plate. 'We can go look for the skeleton . . . if you really want.'

Stanley smiled a little, because Jaxon was an awesome friend, but he knew in his heart it was over. Tracking down the skeleton wouldn't be enough to win the contest. Even if they could catch it, they wouldn't be able to submit a photo before the deadline.

Although the words weighed heavy on his tongue, he said, 'Nah, let's just enjoy the party.'

'Are you sure?'

Stanley paused, but there was no use second-guessing. He'd already made up his mind. 'I'm sure.'

———

The Halloween party was even more epic than Stanley could have imagined. It was the perfect thing to help him forget about the contest.

The best part was when Jaxon's dad let them be monsters in the haunted house. Stanley had his own coffin, and one time when he burst out of it and screamed, this seventh grader from two streets over started crying. The only bad thing about hiding inside a coffin was that it got all hot and stuffy inside, and it gave him time to think about the contest he couldn't possibly win.

So once the crowd died down, Stanley climbed out to see if Jaxon wanted to go in the house for a while and play *Ancient Aliens: Stonehenge Revenge*, but he wasn't there.

Stanley wandered around looking for Jaxon. The party had thinned out by then. A few teenagers huddled in a corner, smoking. A girl screamed, and then the scream turned into snorting laughter. Stanley was about to head over towards the house when someone ran past him and nearly knocked him over. He spun around in time to see a white blur disappear through the gate.

Sweat pricked Stanley's armpits. He knew he'd said he was done with the contest, but something about that blur made him change his mind. He shrugged out of his chest plate and zombie-proof helmet. Footsteps crunched the grass on the other side of the fence. A muggy wind rattled the aluminium gravestones stuck in the garden, but Stanley heard another sound, too. Not like metal vibrating in the breeze. More like bones clinking together in the bottom of a sack.

Stanley ran after the figure, leaving behind the light and warmth of the party for the dark and damp of the ditch behind Jaxon's house.

He caught a glimpse of the shape up ahead. It turned back to look at him, bones glowing yellow in the moonlight. Stanley stamped along the wet concrete until the ditch came to an end. The figure scrambled on to the pavement. A car drove past, and the headlights illuminated a boy, about Stanley's age, wearing a cheap skeleton costume. A group of kids walked by and the boy joined in with them. Stanley slid back into the shadows, feeling stupid and sweaty and out of breath.

The party kind of fizzled after that, and Stanley's mom came to pick him up just before eleven. Stanley didn't tell Jaxon about the kid in the skeleton costume; he felt like too much of an idiot.

Later that night, long after Mom had gone to bed, Stanley crept into the garden. He couldn't sleep knowing the skeleton was still out there somewhere. The image of that white blur streaking past kept playing over and over in his head. And it wasn't even because of the contest. He'd already blown his chances of winning that.

It was because every time he closed his eyes, cold fingers slid around his neck, and he woke up gasping for air. When he drifted into sleep, he imagined he was spiraling down hollow eye sockets full of damp and cold and worms.

Maybe it was just a bad dream, or maybe Jaxon was right. Skeletons didn't just get up and walk away, not outside of scary stories. Dad had always told him the best way to get over being afraid of something was to face it head-on. That meant there was only one thing to do . . . He had to catch the skeleton before the skeleton caught him.

He found a possum family living in the shed behind the broken lawn mower, a dead rat under the tarpaulin covering the grill, and a mouldy Easter egg forgotten in an empty planter.

No skeleton.

The backs of his hands tingled with relief, but he wasn't ready to give up. He climbed over the back fence and dropped down on the other side, trying hard not to think about what he would do if he actually caught something. The grass tickled his belly button. In the silvery moonlight, the field looked like a giant version of Ms Francine's sweater, blowing in the wind.

Stanley slumped down against the fence slats. He wished Jaxon were there. He would know what to do.

'Darby Brothers' rule number eight: Every problem has a solution.' Jaxon's voice echoed in his head.

He thought and thought, and kicked at the ground, and thought some more. Jagged stones came loose under his feet.

That gave him an idea.

He might not be able to find the skeleton in all those

weeds, but maybe he could scare him out. He scooped up a handful of stones and tossed one into the swaying grass.

Nothing.

He threw another rock, a bigger one this time. Something squealed and skittered off towards the trees. He didn't think it sounded like a skeleton. Probably another possum, or a not-so-dead rat. He chucked all of the rocks he could find, one by one, but he never hit anything but the squealer.

After a while, he gave up trying to hit anything and just threw the rocks because he could. Further and further, until one hit a tree at least two hundred feet away with a hollow ping.

Arm sore from throwing, Stanley sighed and climbed back over the fence. The *PixelBlock* T-shirt he'd bought with his Christmas money tore on the way down.

Great.

He stomped up to the spot where the skeleton had grown and kicked it.

'That's for making my little sister cry.' And for turning him into a real-life, sleep-deprived zombie.

To his surprise, his foot dislodged a chunk of soft earth. He bent down and wiggled his fingers into the gooey, wet mud. Now that the skeleton had disappeared, the ground was normal again. He dug around some more and gasped when his fingers hit something hard and cool to the touch.

Tingly sparks lit up his fingertips and ran along the back of his neck. Was it possible there was a second skeleton growing in his garden? Wasn't one creepy monster enough? Stanley tugged on the hard, cool thing, but it wouldn't come loose. He scooped out more mud, and then a light came on in the hole he'd dug.

The iPad screen shone up at him, flashing the time in white letters. 11:59 p.m. The inside of Stanley's mouth went numb. He wrenched the iPad loose and opened up the browser. It was still on the submission page for the Young Discoverer's Prize.

There were a few seconds left to midnight.

Stanley removed the corrupted image file from his entry. Only thirty seconds to go. He found the good version, still saved on the iPad's home screen, and hit the upload button. Twenty seconds. The progress bar crept across the screen. Ten seconds.

'Come on!'

Five.

Four.

Three.

Ping! 'Your photo has been successfully uploaded.'

Stanley sank back into the mud, dizzy with excitement. He stared at the iPad, the screen shaking in his hands, and all he could do was laugh. He laughed and laughed, and when he'd laughed all he could, he did the only other thing he could think of. He headed inside to wash the mud from under his nails. He peeled off his shoes, left them in the cubbyhole next to the door, and then scrubbed his fingers in warm water until the shaking stopped.

He'd done it. He'd entered the contest. He practically ran down the hall, that's how much his body was buzzing, but then he froze. The iPad fell from his hands and dropped on to the puffy carpet.

Lights flickered in Miren's bedroom, purple and gold stars turning dizzy circles on the ceiling. She was probably playing with the glow wand Ms Francine had given her for her birthday, the one with shiny streamers on the end. But that wasn't what freaked Stanley out. It was just an inkling, like a weight slowly pressing him into the carpet, but he knew something wasn't right.

'Mir-Bear, time to go back to sle—'

The words caught in his throat. He stepped into Miren's room and saw the shape looming over her bed . . . not a shape, a skeleton . . . sitting hunchbacked on her mattress, his bony jaw opening wide, his eye sockets empty and suffocating.

'Get away –' Stanley couldn't speak. He stood, helpless, as the skeleton twisted his fingers in the air, and that was when he saw Miren, small and fragile, tucked under her Stripy Pony covers.

'Get away!' Stanley rushed into the room, forcing himself to move. He reached for the skeleton, but Miren's voice stopped him.

She wriggled out of the blanket, rippling with laughter. 'Stanley! Look, it's Stripy Pony!'

'Miren, come over here, now! It's not safe!' Stanley held out his hand, like Miren was drowning and he was trying to rescue her.

'No Butt-Breath, look at the wall.'

Stanley looked at the wall behind Miren's bed. Her glow wand cast a circle of warm light. The skeleton bent his fingers into a complicated shape, and a shadow pony danced across the wall, making circles and leaps and graceful pirouettes.

Miren clapped. Stanley's fists unclenched, and the

ball that had formed in the pit of his stomach started to dissolve.

'Do another one, Princy. Do one for Stanley, even if he is a big Bony-Butt.'

The skeleton wiggled and curled his fingers until another shadow came to life on Miren's wall. A zombie lurched forward, loose skin hanging off his chin. He jumped on a skateboard, then looped around and around an invisible skatepark.

Miren's entire body shook with laughter. Stanley looked at the skeleton, with his knobby cheekbones and skinny fingers. And the skeleton looked at Stanley, but only for a second, before his eye sockets grew wide and his knees started to shake.

'Stop it, Stanley, you're scaring Princy!'

'I'm scaring him?' Some of the nerves that had been pricking under Stanley's skin started to relax. 'Don't you mean the other way around?'

'No, look, he's all sad now. Tell him you like his shadow people. Come on, Stanley! You're going to ruin everything. I want to see more shadow people.'

'Shadow puppets . . . oh, never mind.' He sighed, deep and long. His brain felt like a rubber band being pulled in opposite directions. 'I'm not going to apologize to a skeleton.'

'Please!' Miren craned her neck up at him, lips pushed into a pout.

'Guh, all right, no pouty face.' Stanley couldn't believe what he was about to do. One minute he thought the skeleton was out to kill him; now it was like *he* was the monster. 'Look, Mr Skeleton or whatever . . . I'm sorry . . .'

'It's Princy!' Stanley gave Miren his enough-is-enough big brother look. 'OK, Princy says he's not afraid any more. Come on, Princy, show Stanley some more tricks.'

After Princy made a duck that flapped its wings and did cartwheels, and a dinosaur that knew ballet, Stanley decided that maybe movies didn't get everything right. Princy wasn't scary. He was kind of a wimp, the way he flinched every time Stanley got close to him. But what *was* he? Not a normal skeleton, that was for sure.

'Time for bed,' Stanley said when the clock in the hall chimed one in the morning.

'But Stanley, I want to see more shadow people! And Princy isn't tired, so can't we stay up a little longer? Please?'

'Maybe tomorrow night.' Stanley tucked Miren under the covers and made sure the tubes were still tight in her nose. 'Mom's probably trying to sleep anyway. You know she has to go to work early.'

'I know.' Miren frowned. 'Why does Momma have to work *all* the time now that Daddy's gone?'

'She doesn't work all the time. Come on, let's go back to sleep.'

'You, too?' Miren said.

'Me, too.'

'What about Princy?'

The skeleton shifted uncomfortably in his seat.

'He wants to stay, Stanley. I made a spot for him.'

Miren had set out a doll's pillow and blanket on the floor. They were big enough for Ashleigh, but definitely not for a full-size skeleton.

'I don't think he'll fit.'

'No, he's comfy, see?'

The skeleton curled up on the floor, putting his head on the pint-size pillow and using the blanket to cover his ribs.

'Are you sure you want him to stay?' Stanley said. 'I can stay, too, if you want.'

Miren shook her head. 'Just Princy.'

She yawned, rolled over to face the window, and a few minutes later started to snore. Stanley watched the skeleton a while longer. He couldn't see his eyes any more – they were facing the wall – but his ribs seemed to rise and fall under the glittery blanket.

CHAPTER TWENTY

Stanley woke up Sunday morning to the sound of laughter and the smell of sizzling bacon. To his surprise, he hadn't had any more nightmares about hollow eye sockets or bony fingers. Instead, he'd dreamed about shadow zombies performing a ballet, and how he and Miren and even Princy got up onstage and danced with them.

It was a weird dream.

Then he remembered the contest. He bolted out of bed to check the entries. A lot of people had submitted photos at the last minute. There were seventy-four entries in all, but his was back at number one. One thousand three hundred

and twenty-six likes! And, better yet, the photo was still there.

'The winner will be chosen by a panel of experts from *National Geographic* magazine. Our experts will meet with the top three finalists to analyse their discoveries in person before making their final decision. Thank you for your patience as we review your submissions.'

'Now the oranges!' Stanley heard Miren shout from in the kitchen. 'Stanley, come and look! He's doing the oranges!'

Stanley tried to stand up, but his bones suddenly felt like lead. Why hadn't he thought of it before? Of course they would want to see his discovery in person. And what would happen when the people from *National Geographic* came to his house and saw Princy doing shadow puppets? That is, if they could see him in the first place.

Stanley staggered into the kitchen, his brain a tangle of confused thoughts. He blinked like his eyes needed a minute to adjust, as he saw Princy sitting cross-legged on the dining room floor, juggling apples and bananas and oranges.

'Little Stanley, you're awake. About time, too. In

Kyrgyzstan, we always got up before the sun to milk the goats.'

'We don't have any goats,' he said through numb lips.

'This is true. Here.' Ms Francine handed Stanley a spatula. 'Go flip the bacon.'

'What's *he* doing here?' Stanley said, nodding to the skeleton. Maybe it was a weird question to ask, considering he was the one who'd discovered him, but it didn't seem right for him to be sitting in the dining room like it was no big deal. 'Does Mom know he's here?'

'What do you think?' Ms Francine tilted her head at him.

'She still can't see him, can she?'

'Not yet,' said Ms Francine.

'He looks strange sitting there like that.'

The skeleton stopped mid-juggle. Two apples and a banana clattered down on his head.

'Shush! You'll hurt his feelings, little Stanley.' Ms Francine pulled him aside. 'You don't want to scare him away. See how he makes your sister happy?'

Stanley watched the skeleton pick up the fruit and start to juggle again. No, he didn't want to scare the skeleton away, did he? What if the experts from *National*

Geographic came and there was no skeleton? Still, it was strange, even if every time the skeleton looked at Stanley, his cavernous eyes went wide. Geez, who'd ever seen a scaredy-cat skeleton?

And there was something else. Miren. Her face lit up as the skeleton juggled. He made her happy, like Ms Francine said. She clapped and bobbed her feet and didn't seem to notice the tubes or the tank.

'I guess he's OK.' Stanley turned to the stove and nudged the crackling strips. 'But I'm not saving him any bacon.'

'I don't think he'll mind,' Ms Francine said. 'Now, you two eat fast, because today Ms Francine is taking you on an adventure.'

———

'Why can't Princy come with us? He was going to show me some new dance moves.' Miren smooshed her face against the bus window. 'Today won't be any fun without Princy!'

'Like my Uncle Goat always used to say,' said Ms Francine, 'some people need ten goats to be happy. Me, all I need is the mountainside.'

'That doesn't make any sense,' Stanley said.

'Your uncle is a goat?' Miren laughed.

'Yes and no. Uncle Goat was his nickname, but he did have hair, just here.' Ms Francine rubbed her bristly chin. 'It's better to have the mountainside, because then the goats will come to you. Patience, little one.' She patted Miren's head and looked at her with sad eyes. Stanley didn't understand why she looked so sad.

Twenty-eight minutes later, according to Stanley's *PixelBlock* watch, the bus stopped outside the Museum of Natural History.

'Come on, little ones. Hurry up, quickly.'

On the pavement in front of the museum, a dinosaur statue towered over them.

'Look, Stanley, that dinosaur's bigger than outer space. Why's his head so weird?' Miren took Stanley's hand. Somehow, Ms Francine's story about the goat had seemed to cheer her up.

'That,' Ms Francine said, 'is a life-size replica of a brachiosaur. The tallest dinosaur ever discovered.'

'Whoa.' Stanley's eyes travelled all the way up the neck to the knobby head on top. Why couldn't he have found something normal like that?

'Like you say, whoa.' The word sounded funny in

Ms Francine's mouth. 'Now, follow me. We have many bones to see and not so much time to see them.'

She nudged Stanley and Miren up the stairs and through the heavy front doors. Stanley carried Miren's tank as they climbed a massive staircase to the second storey. Along the way, she blew a kiss to each of the bronze monkeys dangling from the railing.

They came out into an atrium. Another dinosaur skeleton greeted them at the top, hunched forward like it was ready to charge.

'Triceratops!' Stanley said. He picked up Miren's tank so they could run to the rope barrier surrounding the bones.

'I like his pointy nose.' Miren laughed. 'Very fancy.'

'That's a horn,' Stanley said. 'The name triceratops means three horns.'

Ms Francine led them through rooms of polished display cases packed with old bones. A woolly mammoth with curly tusks ate leaves from a tree in one display. There was an entire room dedicated to ancient sharks. The whole time, Stanley wondered if any of the archaeologists at the museum had ever tried to dig up bones, only to have them get up and walk away. Maybe, but he didn't think so.

The third floor featured an exhibit called *Human Bodies Revealed*.

'These people gave their bodies to science after they died. So others could learn from them,' said Ms Francine.

'You mean they're real?' Stanley said.

Miren reached her fingers out towards an old man hunched over a cane. Stanley could see the muscles and bones splayed out underneath his skin.

'Go ahead,' Ms Francine said. 'This display says it's OK to touch.'

Miren poked a flap of dried skin, and a tiny shiver ran through her body and into Stanley's fingers.

Stanley wondered what it would be like to live in a museum after he died. The idea made his brain go all wobbly. Would he be able to watch the people passing through the museum? Could he flick them in the nose if they got too close, like Princy?

Or would he turn to dust and crumbled-up bones? Unable to look or think or feel? Nothing but an empty space.

Stanley stopped at the foot of a body posed with one leg cocked back. He looked frozen in time, like any second he might snap to life and kick an invisible ball across the room. Stanley touched his bony wrist and then wished he hadn't. It felt fake, like plastic.

A group of students in grey-and-blue uniforms filed out of the exhibit, leaving Stanley, Miren, and Ms Francine alone. They sat in a mini-theatre and watched a movie about how the travelling bodies got preserved before they went on their world tour. Miren's eyes grew bigger by the second. Stanley clutched his forehead, and the room started to spin.

'Let's go get a cold drink,' Ms Francine said when the movie finished. Maybe she could tell Stanley was about to throw up. 'What would you say to a drink and some dinosaur tracks ice cream in the museum restaurant?'

'Yay! Is it made of real dinosaurs?' Miren jumped up and down. It was a good thing Stanley was carrying her tank, or she probably would have tipped it over again. Stanley started to answer, but Miren said, 'Just kidding. What do you think I am, a dummy?'

They were heading towards the exit when Stanley saw something odd out of the corner of his eye. One of the bodies in the *Human Bodies Revealed* exhibit didn't have any skin or muscle left on its bones. It was the only one like that. Stanley was surprised he hadn't noticed it before.

'Hold on a minute, Mir-Bear.' He stopped to get a better look, and that was when the skull spun around and a black eye socket winked at him.

'Princy, you came!'

Miren rushed over to the skeleton and gave him a bone-crushing hug. It was all Stanley could do to keep up with her.

'I just knew you would come,' Miren said. 'We saw woolly elephants and dinos and a big mean shark the size of two sharks! Also, we're going to eat real dinosaur ice cream, can you believe it? Just kidding, hey, where's your hat?'

The skeleton twirled in place and then dropped into a low bow. Miren clapped. Just then, a second school group, in red-and-black uniforms, pounded up the stairs. Stanley and Miren turned around, and when they looked back, the skeleton had gone.

'Oh no, Princy! Those dodo brains scared him off.'

Stanley searched the display, but he found no sign of Princy. Ugh, that name. There was no getting around it. He was going to have to start calling the skeleton by his vomit-inducing name.

'Too bad, very sad.' Ms Francine shrugged. 'That was a nice surprise for you, little one, but I'm sure you'll see him again when we get home. Now, we'd better go. We don't want to keep this ice cream waiting.'

Miren thought about it. Stanley could tell she was close to bursting into tears.

'Ice cream with sprinkles and chocolate chip cookies on top?' Stanley added.

Miren sighed. 'OK, I guess so.'

Stanley laughed, but only on the outside. Inside, his brain was a ball of knots. Ms Francine picked up Miren and her tank, and they headed back towards the stairs. Stanley took one last look at the exhibit before they left. For a second, he thought he saw one of the skulls on the 'Humans through History' wall turn to him and smile.

He should have been freaked out. He *was* freaked out, but in another way seeing Princy in the museum made him feel better. Like maybe death wasn't all worms and nothingness. Maybe, sometimes, there was mystery and whimsy and dancing shadow puppets, too. The kind that needed both light and dark to be seen.

'Come on, Stanley. Ice cream time.'

'Wait up.' He hurried after Miren and Ms Francine. 'Last one to ice cream's a rotten nobody!'

CHAPTER TWENTY-ONE

On the way home, they got off the bus outside the two-storey Walgreens where Mom worked.

'A surprise for Momma,' Ms Francine said.

They bought white flowers at the newsstand, and Miren picked out a copy of *Dog Fancy*, Mom's favourite. They found Mom restocking baby oil in aisle seven.

'Look who it is!' Her cracked lips lifted into a smile. She kissed Miren's forehead. 'You seem like you've been having fun.'

Miren told Mom all about the dinos and the

muscly people and the chocolate chip gummy bear ice cream that had taken her forty-five minutes to eat.

'I had a bite or two,' said Ms Francine.

'That sounds wonderful.'

Mom walked them down the aisles and showed them the new specials. Ben and Jerry's, two for five dollars. Stanley's stomach grumbled. His ice cream had been even bigger than Miren's, topped with brownie batter, icing, and mini Reese's cups. He was beginning to regret eating the whole thing.

'Stanley, can you show Miren the toy aisle? I need to talk to Ms Francine,' Mom said, in a tone that made Stanley think he hadn't been listening the first time she'd said it.

'OK, Mom.'

'Look, Stanley. A Hula-Hoop and one of those whoopee things that sounds like a fart. I could really use one of those.'

'For what?'

'For school, obviously.'

Stanley didn't ask any more questions. He pushed Miren's tank and listened to her talk about the toys. He also strained to hear what Mom and Ms Francine were saying on the other side of the shelves.

'I'm afraid that a big outing like this is too much excitement for her. The doctors said she needs her rest.'

'She's a little girl, dochka. Let her see the world. What do these doctors know about such things?'

'I'm her mother, and I think I know what's best for her. I just want her to get better.'

'I know, little one, I know.'

'Stanley, pay attention! Should I get the squishy ball or the doll with a horsey tail?'

'It's a ponytail, and I don't think Mom's going to get you anything. Not after you just had your birthday.'

'Dumb birthday.' Miren stamped her foot and tossed the ball and the doll back on the shelf. 'Ooh, colouring books!'

Stanley put the toys back where they belonged and peeked over the top of the shelf to see if Mom and Ms Francine were done talking. Mom was blowing her nose into a tissue. Ms Francine patted her on the back, but Mom pulled away. Stanley couldn't hear what they were saying any more, but he did see something in the security mirror hanging just behind Mom's head.

Something white.

Stanley whirled and saw a head slip behind the shelf on the other side. It was Princy – Stanley was sure of it.

He raced to the next aisle and glimpsed a white heel vanish behind a display of orange juice. He ran after it, but when he got to the end, there was nothing.

'Grandpa, look, a bone man!'

Stanley followed the voice to the pharmacy counter. A boy in overalls pointed at the blood pressure chair. 'See, Grandpa, bone man! Like at Halloween.'

The grandad lifted up his glasses and squinted at the chair. 'Sorry, kiddo, old peepers aren't what they used to be.'

'Brandon, look, a bone man! Bone man!'

He flicked an older boy on the elbow. Brandon flung a tuft of purple hair out of his eyes and said, 'That's just a dummy, dummy.' He slipped headphones into his ears and started to bob his head to the music.

'Bone man!' the little boy cried, and he flopped on to the floor, kicking and screaming. 'Why won't you listen to me!'

Stanley gaped at Princy, and Princy gaped back. When the little boy wasn't looking, Princy winked and then disappeared through a door marked MAINTENANCE CUPBOARD, AUTHORIZED PERSONNEL ONLY. Stanley ran after him. It was one thing for him to turn up in a museum, but why had he followed them here? He was just about to open the door when Mom came up behind him and grabbed his shoulder.

'You were supposed to be watching Miren! She can't pull the tank by herself, you know that. What if someone had taken her? What if she had fallen? God, Stanley, what were you thinking?'

Mom's fingernails dug into Stanley's skin. He opened his mouth, but he didn't know what to say. He couldn't understand why Mom was so mad.

'I'm taking you home right now, all of you.' She shot a glance at Ms Francine.

'Is Stanley in trouble?' Miren said. 'But Momma, we were just playing hide-and-seek. Right, Stanley?'

Stanley couldn't believe his ears, but Mom wasn't buying it. 'Stanley should have known better.'

'Stella, what are you doing? You were supposed to take over for me five minutes ago!' A thin man with greasy hair and a Walgreens vest came up behind Mom. 'This isn't a day care centre. How many times do I have to tell you that? Now, either get to the counter and start ringing people up, or pack your stuff. Got it?'

Mom's lips drew into a tight line. 'Got it.'

Inside, Stanley's stomach boiled. He'd never heard someone talk to his mom like that before. If Dad were still here, he probably would have punched the guy in the face.

Mom waited for the greasy man to walk out of earshot before she said to Ms Francine, 'You get them home right now. No more adventures. We'll talk about next week when I get off work. But I can tell you right now, we may not need your services any more.'

'Mom!' Stanley said, but her expression shut him up fast.

'As for you.' She dragged her hands over her forehead. 'I'm too angry to talk to you right now.' She started to walk away. Her chest heaved and her cheeks burned red. 'You know what? You'd better be asleep by the time I get home, because I don't even want to see your face.'

The words cut deep into Stanley's chest.

'What did I do?' Stanley said to Mom's back. But it was too late; she was already gone.

'She doesn't mean it,' Ms Francine said once they got outside, but Stanley wasn't so sure. 'She's just worried about little sister. Worry makes people say funny things.'

On the bus ride home, Stanley wished Dad was there more than ever. Mom had never yelled at him or Ms Francine like that when Dad was around. Probably because she had so much less to worry about.

Miren fell asleep with her head on Stanley's shoulder. He stared out of the window, ignoring Ms Francine's story about the goat and the chicken who had a fight, but then made up when it came time to trick the farmer. He knew it was supposed to make him feel better, but he wasn't in the mood.

One thought kept playing over and over in his head, like the repeating background in the video game *Super Mushroom Smash*. This whole thing was Princy's fault. Stupid skeleton. If it hadn't been for him, none of this would have happened. Maybe Jaxon had been right about Princy after all.

CHAPTER TWENTY-TWO

Stanley went straight to his room when he got home and slammed the door. He didn't come out when Ms Francine called for dinner, or even later when she made peanut butter cookies from the tube.

Instead, he put on his headphones and got online to play *Ancient Aliens Attack!* He'd just blasted seven Martian slugs in a row when a voice shouted in his ear.

'Stanley! You're not going to believe this, but the photo's back!'

Jaxon had logged on to *Ancient Aliens Attack!* and was talking to him through his headphones. 'Hey, are you there? You're back at the top of the ratings. You could really win this thing.'

'Um, not exactly,'

Stanley said, feeling the way he sometimes did right before he had to throw up.

He told Jaxon everything, about finding the iPad in the garden, the shadow puppets, even how Princy had followed them to the museum and Walgreens. 'What will the judges think when they see Princy juggling and running around the house?'

'Ha! You're calling him Princy now. I knew that would happen.' Jaxon's voice crackled in Stanley's ear. Mom had promised to get him a new pair of headphones for his birthday, but now he doubted she'd ever buy him anything again. 'Stanley?'

'Yeah?'

White noise buzzed and popped on the other end. 'I need to do more research. It's just, I've never heard about something like this happening before. And I've read all one hundred and forty-eight Darby Brothers' mysteries.'

'What do you mean?'

'I mean the contest isn't the only thing you should be worried about.'

'I told you, he's a wimp. He was so scared he was shaking.'

'Still . . .' Jaxon paused for so long, Stanley thought

his headphones might have gone out completely. 'Look, I'll read up more on it tonight, and you can meet me in the library before first period. Do you think you can catch the early bus tomorrow?'

'Definitely,' Stanley said. He wanted to get out of the house before Mom woke up anyway, and this would give him an excuse. 'Oh, by the way, sorry about your iPad. It's kind of a wreck.'

'It's no big deal. Mom says she's going to buy me the new one that just came out anyway.'

'Oh.'

'Besides, we have bigger problems than an old iPad.' Over the buzzing sound, Stanley could almost hear Jaxon clicking his jaw back and forth the way he did when he got nervous. 'Do you want to sleep over at my house tonight? I mean you and Miren and your mom? We have enough room.'

'What? Why would we do that?' said Stanley. Jaxon didn't answer. 'Oh, because of him.'

'Yeah. Him,' Jaxon said.

'No, we'll be fine. I told you, he's a wimp.'

'Just think about it, OK?'

'Trust me. Besides, maybe it won't be so bad having him around.'

'Just promise you won't do anything stupid,' said Jaxon.

'Like what?'

'Like trying to get Princy to sit still while a bunch of experts from *National Geographic* examine him.'

'I'm not that crazy,' Stanley said, and he was almost sure he meant it.

'OK, I'll see you tomorrow. And Stanley?'

'Yeah?'

'Be careful.'

The headphones clicked as DarbyFan#1 logged off the game. Stanley had been so busy talking that an alien had exploded his eyeball with a laser gun and another had covered his moon fort in slime. He shut down his computer, flipped off the lights, and climbed into bed.

He closed his eyes, expecting more dreams of dancing shadow zombies, but instead Princy's hollowed-out skull turned to him and smiled. It wasn't a scary smile, exactly, but Stanley still couldn't fall asleep.

He tried to count backwards from one hundred, like Mom always told him. When that didn't work, he pretended to count goats jumping over an imaginary fence, Ms Francine's idea. No luck. He kept picturing a white skeleton hand shooting up and catching the goats by the ankle.

Three hours and eleven minutes later, according to his light-up Abominable Zombie alarm clock, Stanley heard voices whispering at the end of the hall. He sat up in bed, figuring Mom must finally be home from work. He pressed his ear to the crack in the door to try to hear what she was saying. Only Mom wasn't the one talking – it was Miren. And the voice that answered her back was like none he had ever heard before.

Sand scraping against old bones.

Stanley turned his doorknob, ready to run down the hall and rescue Miren, but then he heard the garage door open. A few seconds later, Mom tapped into the kitchen, and the voices went quiet. She turned on the sink, and then the microwave clicked shut.

Stanley listened to see if the voices would come back, but all he heard was the late-night talk show Mom was watching in the living room. He crawled back into bed, but this time he didn't bother counting goats. No way he was falling asleep tonight.

CHAPTER TWENTY-THREE

The next morning, Stanley caught the early bus. It was still dark out, but the bus was full of people in business suits heading into the city. Stanley got off a block from school and pushed through the drizzle and wind all the way up to the front doors.

He found Jaxon hunched over a book in the back corner of the library. The book was about the same size as Jaxon, with a velvety red cover.

'You're not gonna like this,' Jaxon said, clutching the page he'd just been reading to his chest.

'Show me,' Stanley said. He was tired and grumpy and not in the mood for games.

Jaxon chewed the inside of his mouth. 'OK, but don't say I didn't warn you.' He turned the book around so Stanley could see a painting of a skeleton holding a stick with a crescent-shaped blade on the end. Strands of flesh hung from his bones, and he stood atop a pile of mangled bodies, all with their eyes closed.

'That thing he's holding is called a scythe,' Jaxon said. 'He uses it to gather the souls of the dead. Look familiar?'

Stanley nodded, but he wasn't really listening. He was too busy staring at the velvety cloak draped over the skeleton's head.

'Who is he?' Stanley said, working hard to keep his voice from shaking.

'The Grim Reaper.' Jaxon looked around, like he was worried someone might be spying on them. For all Stanley knew, someone, or something, probably was. 'His job is to bring the dead to the other side. They say he only appears when someone is –' The last part caught in Jaxon's throat.

'Just say it,' Stanley said, thinking of Miren lying in that hospital bed.

'When someone is dying.'

Jaxon checked out the big book, and every time he ran into Stanley he told him more facts about the Grim Reaper. But it didn't matter; Stanley had already heard all he needed to know. Princy, or whatever his real name was, was up to no good. Even if he did smile and dance and act like a wimp. When Stanley got home, he was going to find Princy and make sure he left Miren alone. Scythe or no scythe.

Stanley hurried straight home after school. He'd called Ms Francine at lunch, so he knew Mom wouldn't be back until late. Good, because when Stanley got his hands on Princy, things weren't going to be pretty.

He found the front door locked. He rang the doorbell, but nobody answered, so he used his key to get in. The lawn mower hummed in the garden. Ms Francine was the only old lady he'd ever met who loved mowing lawns.

'Mir-Bear,' he called. 'Come on out. I need to talk to you about something.'

Miren didn't answer, but he could hear her coughing. He ran to her bedroom. Miren lay curled up on the bed, hands wrapped around her throat. She gasped and wheezed for air. Stanley pressed the tubes into her nose, but they were already tight. The little dial on the oxygen tank was spinning, but Miren still couldn't breathe.

'Ms Francine!' Stanley screamed.

That was when Stanley saw the white skull peeking over the edge of Miren's bed. Two shadowy eye sockets blazed into his brain, just like the ones in the library book. Stanley lunged. His fingers grazed a knobby vertebra, but Princy was too fast.

He disappeared under Miren's bed. Stanley grabbed for him, found something hard, and tugged. It was Stripy Pony. Stanley ducked down and stared at the space under the bed. He couldn't believe his eyes. It was empty, except for some dirty socks and the set of pink gardening tools.

Miren's coughing grew louder and then stopped. Her body went still.

'Ms Francine!' Stanley screamed again.

Then he remembered that she couldn't hear him because of the mower. Ice shot up Stanley's spine and froze his insides.

'Miren, wake up!' He shook her tiny shoulders, but her eyes didn't open. 'Ms Francine!'

Stanley didn't know what else to do, so he stumbled into the kitchen and dialled 9-1-1.

CHAPTER TWENTY-FOUR

Stanley and Ms Francine rode in the back of the ambulance while men in blue vests hooked Miren up to machines and pressed on her rib cage. Stanley squeezed Ms Francine's fingers so tight he thought they might break. But they didn't, and Ms Francine squeezed back even harder.

'Your momma will be worried sick,' she said. 'A mother always is when something has happened to her little one.'

Everything in the ambulance was shiny metal, buzzing machines, and hard white plastic. It made Stanley feel like he was travelling in a spaceship, and any minute they would crash into some frozen, uninhabitable planet.

Wheels screeched as they pulled into the hospital. People in scrubs wheeled Miren down a hallway and into a room with flapping doors.

'You have to stay outside,' a nurse said to Stanley.

She pushed him in the chest so he wouldn't follow, and that was how he ended up in a waiting room with too-bright lights and seats that smelt like rubbing alcohol. Ms Francine sat down next to him and cupped a hand around his cheek. Her skin was so flaky and rough it felt like scales.

Stanley blinked away the headache threatening to blossom behind his left eye. Ms Francine took back her hand and pulled the silver locket out from under her blouse. The one she always wore. She unclasped the heart with bent fingers and showed Stanley the pictures inside.

'You and your dad,' Stanley said, remembering the last time she'd shown him. 'Did he really die playing chess . . . like you said?' He could hardly speak for fear of being sick.

'That is true.' She rubbed a finger over the edge of the locket. 'And you know what? Believe it or not, he was happy when he went. I was little, so I didn't know that death always had to be sad and terrible and something to fight against. I watched Papa's face the moment the light went out of it. And do you know what he did?' Stanley shook his head. 'He smiled.'

'And who was playing chess with him?' Stanley asked. He couldn't understand it, but he thought he knew the answer, and it made his eyeball throb.

'This one and that one.'

'No, tell me.' The words came out sharp, like their jagged edges might cut anyone who heard them.

Ms Francine didn't seem to notice. 'Love is a funny thing. Sometimes it is long and slow and rolling. A lazy river of love. Other times, it's over so fast you blink and you might miss it. Both things are love, Stanley. Don't forget that.'

'It was him, wasn't it?' Stanley balled his fists in his lap. 'The skeleton? He was the one your dad was playing when he died.'

Ms Francine snapped the locket shut and dropped it down inside her blouse. 'Let's go find Momma,' she said.

They met Mom at the emergency entrance. She hugged Stanley so tight he couldn't breathe. Ms Francine tried to lead Mom down the hall to the waiting room, but Mom insisted on talking to the doctors, the nurses, anyone who would listen.

Go, Mom!

'We'll let you know as soon as we hear something. She's in a critical state right now, Ms Stanwright. The best thing you can do, the only thing you can do, is wait. Do you understand? You have to wait.' The nurse helped Mom into a chair in the waiting room, where she looked up at Stanley and Ms Francine with uncomprehending eyes. 'Why is this happening?'

She pulled Stanley into the chair next to her and cried into his hair. Stanley wrapped his arms around her and he cried, too, just a little.

'I'm so sorry, Stanley,' she said once she'd soaked Stanley's hair with her tears. 'I didn't mean what I said yesterday, not any of it. I love you, you know that, right?'

Stanley nodded, but his throat hurt too much to say anything.

'You are a good momma,' Ms Francine said. She sat

across from Mom, their knees touching.

'And I'm sorry about what I said to you, Belka. I don't know what we'd do without you.'

'It's OK.' Ms Francine swatted the air. 'I have thick skin. Everyone in Kyrgyzstan is like this. You live through seven months of winter with no heat and only a wool blanket to keep you warm, you would have thick skin, too.'

The tip of Mom's mouth tilted up, and then a doctor in a white coat came around the corner. 'Ms Stanwright?'

'Yes, I'm Ms Stanwright.' Mom stood up, and so did Stanley. 'Is she OK?'

'Your daughter is breathing normally, but we need to keep her for observation. We're not sure why her lungs keep filling with fluid, but we think—'

'When can I see her?' Mom interrupted.

'Right now, but I do need to talk with you about your daughter's condition.'

'After I see her.'

'I understand. Follow me.'

Miren had been moved to a room in another wing. The room had cheery pink wallpaper and sheets covered in teddy bears. But that didn't fool Stanley. He saw the machines and the tubes hooked to Miren's wrist.

A mask covered her mouth. Her eyelids fluttered when Mom said her name, but she didn't open her eyes.

'She won't wake up tonight,' the doctor said, 'if the medicine does its job.'

Mom brushed the hair from Miren's cheek. 'I love you,' she whispered, and she bent down to kiss her earlobe.

'When you're ready, Ms Stanwright, we can discuss Miren's medical needs.'

'In the hallway, I don't want . . . Let's just go out into the hallway.'

Stanley started to follow, but Ms Francine held him back. 'Your momma needs to do this alone. She wants to protect you.'

'I don't need protection. I need to help. Miren's my responsibility, too.'

'I know, you're an old man, am I right? Many responsibilities. But your momma wants to feel like she can still be your momma. You see what I mean?'

'I guess.' Stanley sat down in the chair next to Miren's bed and put his hand on her arm. Her skin felt cold and damp, like she'd been playing outside in the rain.

Mom came back into the room a few minutes later. She forced a smile on to her face when she saw Stanley.

He could tell it was forced, because her eyes looked red like she'd been crying again.

'What did the doctor say?' said Ms Francine.

She shook her head and her smile crumpled. 'They don't know.'

'You can tell me, Mom. I'm not a little kid any more.'

'Of course you're not.' She kneeled beside Stanley and took his hands in hers. 'I promise I would tell you if they knew anything, but they don't. It's serious, that's all the doctor would say, but they haven't been able to determine what's causing it.'

She buried her head in Stanley's side, and a rock dropped down into the pit of his stomach. Mom and the doctors might not know what was making Miren sick, but Stanley did.

CHAPTER TWENTY-FIVE

Ms Francine brought up dinner from the hospital cafeteria. They ate boiled chicken and mashed potatoes, machines whirring in the background. Ms Francine wanted to stay the night, but Mom insisted on driving her home.

'Are you sure you'll be OK by yourself?' Mom said.

'I want to stay with Miren,' Stanley said.

'You're a good big brother.'

Really, he needed to stay to make sure Princy didn't come back, but he didn't say that to Mom.

After she was gone, Stanley curled up in the comfy chair next to Miren's bed and read her stories from the only book he had, *Pigmen Attack! A PixelBlock Adventure.*

'And then,' Stanley yawned, 'Phil mined enough diamond ore to forge a diamond sword. He waited for night to fall. This time, when the zombies came, he would be ready.'

Stanley blinked. He was determined to stay awake. He wished he had a diamond sword, like Phil, the hero of *PixelBlock.* Then, the next time Princy showed his face, that skeleton wouldn't stand a chance. He thought about calling Dad on the hospital phone, but he wouldn't be able to do anything tonight anyway. Not when he was fifteen hundred miles away. No, this stakeout was Stanley's responsibility.

He kept reading. A few minutes later, the words went streaky at the edges. He blinked. He wasn't going to fall asleep. No way. Not when he had to . . . protect . . . Miren.

The next thing Stanley knew, he woke to the sound of rattling bones. He shot up in his chair, hitting his head on the edge of a table.

'Agh!' He staggered to his feet and searched the room. Someone had turned out the lights, and Mom still wasn't back from dropping off Ms Francine. 'Show your face, you stupid skeleton!'

Something squeaked in the bathroom behind him. Light peeked under the door.

'I know you're in there.'

He picked up an empty vase from the table and crept to the side of the door. He flattened himself against the wall, so Princy wouldn't see him until it was too late.

The door opened. Stanley got ready to crash the vase down on Princy's stupid bones.

'Stanley, oh my god, you scared me to death. Why are you holding a vase?'

Mom stepped out of the bathroom, drying her hands on a paper towel.

'I . . .' He wiped the sleep from his eyes. 'I thought I heard someone.'

'Sorry, honey, I didn't mean to scare you, but you were sleeping when I came in. You looked so peaceful I didn't want to wake you.' She kissed him on the forehead. 'I shouldn't have let you stay by yourself. I'm so sorry, but I haven't been thinking straight lately, not with everything going on.'

'No, Mom, I was fine. I just thought I heard someone else, that's all.'

She looked in Stanley's eyes for a long time, biting her lower lip. He thought she was going to say more mushy I love you stuff, but instead she asked him to help her lay out the sleeping bags and blankets she'd brought from home.

When they were done, Stanley crawled into his sleeping bag. So many questions buzzed around his head, but he didn't know how to ask any of them. He tried to close his eyes, but now that Mom was back, he couldn't sleep.

'Mom, do you think we can get flowers for Miren tomorrow? So the vase won't be empty.'

'Sure, baby. But the doctor says we should be going home in the morning. They just wanted to monitor her overnight.'

Silence stretched between them, filled only by machine noises.

'Is Miren going to die?' Stanley said.

He said it so quietly, and Mom took so long to answer, he wasn't sure she'd even heard.

'No,' she said finally. 'She's going to be OK, baby. I promise.'

A sticky hand slapped Stanley awake the next morning.

'Look, Stanley, I got sticky hands. Just like at Dr Cynthia's.'

Miren wielded two sticky hands like nunchucks. They smacked Stanley in the nose and mouth and ear. He should have been mad, but he was so happy to see her feeling better, he couldn't stop smiling.

'Miren, pack up your toys. It's time to go,' Mom said.

'Oookay.'

Miren stopped her assault and stuffed her new toys into a hospital gift bag.

'When did you get all of those?' Stanley said, picking crust from his eyes.

'Mom took me to the shop while you were sleeping. Sleepyhead!'

Miren made up a sleepyhead song about Stanley, and she sang it on the way downstairs and most of the ride home. They stopped at McDonald's to get egg-and-cheese sandwiches.

'And ice cream!' Miren said.

'Just this once.'

Mom ordered Miren a chocolate sundae, and Stanley got a Butterfinger McFlurry. Mom's phone buzzed the whole drive home, but she ignored it.

'You should answer it,' Stanley said. 'It might be Dad.'

Mom just shook her head.

Ms Francine greeted them at the front door with a pot of tea and a plate of warm cookies.

'You didn't have to do that,' Mom said.

Her phone buzzed again in her pocket.

'Go on, talk to your phone already. I'll make sure the little ones eat plenty of cookies.'

'Yay!' Miren fist-pumped the air, just like always.

Stanley helped Miren into her favourite chair at the dining table, the one with the Stripy Pony sticker on the seat.

'Cookies and ice cream! I should go to the hospital more often. Right, Stanley?'

Stanley didn't answer. Miren dumped her bag of toys on to the table and started swatting place mats with her two sticky hands.

Mom came back into the kitchen, her jaw muscles tense. Stanley could always tell when she was worried about something, because her jawbones stuck out in front of her ears.

'I have to go in to work,' Mom said.

'Was it Dad on the phone?'

'Look, Mom, sticky hand is eating cookies. Yum, yum.' Miren crumbled up a cookie with a sticky hand. Pieces of it stuck to the goo and others fell to the floor around Miren's feet.

'Try to keep your cookies on the table.' Mom sighed. She kissed Miren's head and turned to Ms Francine. 'I'm really sorry, but the general manager is in today, and he's been trying to get in touch with me. I just need to go in for a few minutes and tell him I have to take some time off.'

'We're good here, go, go. Don't worry about us. We will have some nice hot borscht waiting when Momma comes home, right, little ones?'

Stanley and Miren groaned.

Ms Francine clucked her tongue. 'You go now, Momma. We'll try not to have too much fun without you. And no more big adventures.'

Mom left for work. Stanley felt stupid for thinking it might have been Dad on the phone. When Miren was finished smearing her cookies all over the table, Stanley helped Ms Francine clean up.

'No school today, then?' said Ms Francine.

'I need to look after Miren.'

'What do your teachers say about this?'

Stanley shrugged.

Miren went to her room to watch an episode of *Stripy Pony: Ponies in Ponytown*. Stanley checked under her bed and inside her wardrobe to make sure Princy wasn't hiding anywhere, but there was no sign of him.

Stanley sat at the dining room table and did his homework. He wanted to go check on his entry for the Young Discoverer's Prize, but Ms Francine wouldn't stop pestering him. While he worked, Ms Francine called someone from the phone book to come and mow the front garden. She was probably scared to do it herself after everything that had happened. Maybe she didn't trust Stanley to take care of Miren by himself.

'You did a good job yesterday,' she said, reading his thoughts. 'Calling 9-1-1. Who taught you to do this?'

'I don't know, school, I guess.'

'Ah, so this school is not so bad, then?'

'It's OK. I just want to stay home with Miren. She needs me.'

'You're a good boy,' Ms Francine said. 'When you finish this page, you can go do your game or whatever boys do nowadays.'

'Thanks!'

Stanley hurried through the last few problems. When he was done, he went to check on Miren. She'd fallen asleep on the floor, on top of her Stripy Pony duvet. When he was sure she was safe, he hurried to his room and pulled up the page for the Young Discoverer's Prize. His entry had almost two thousand likes, and there was a new message on the home page about the contest.

'So far, our judges are highly impressed with the quality of this year's discoveries. Due to the large number of entries, it may take longer than usual for the winner to be announced. Be patient, and remember to check back soon for more updates.'

Great.

Stanley closed the page and opened up a new email to his dad.

'Dad, Miren is really sick. She . . .' Stanley stopped and deleted the last word. '*We* need you to come and help. I'm not sure we can get through this without you.'

Before he had time to think about it, he pushed send.

His lips felt numb as he shoved headphones into his ears and logged on to *Skatepark Zombie Death Bash*. He killed an entire horde of zombie golfers and a circus full of zombie clowns. He smashed zombie after zombie, his teeth digging into his lip. Why did he get so nervous emailing his dad? It wasn't like he was some stranger. Except, after the past ten months, he kind of was.

And maybe emailing him wasn't the scary part. It was the thought of what it would mean if Dad didn't email him back.

He destroyed three more zombie villages before he got tired of raiding and went to find Ms Francine in the kitchen, chopping cabbage.

'Ah, my helper. Good, go and peel these beetroots. Be careful with the peeler, it's sharp. Wouldn't want Momma to find any missing fingers.'

Stanley rolled his eyes, but he took the peeler anyway and attacked the beetroots. Ms Francine turned on some music in a language Stanley didn't understand. He thought it might be Russian.

When he was done with all of the beetroots, he scraped the shavings into the bin and washed the red stains from his fingers.

'I'm going to check on Miren,' Stanley said.

'What?' Ms Francine said. 'I can't hear so well over the music.'

He pointed towards the hall.

'OK, yes, you go. Play your game. Thank you for the help, little Stanley.'

Stanley went down the hall to Miren's room. As he got closer, he could hear that she was giggling. The music was so loud he hadn't noticed it before. His stomach twisted. He looked around for some kind of weapon, but he didn't see anything.

'Do it again,' Miren said.

Stanley ran into her room. He didn't need a weapon; he could take Princy on bare-handed. Stupid, wimpy skeleton.

Princy whirled a rubber ball atop his finger.

'Faster, faster!' Miren jumped up and down on her bed, the oxygen tank bouncing right along with her.

'Stop that!' Stanley shouted. 'You get away from her!'

He shoved Princy into the wall. Bones cracked. Miren stopped bouncing and her mouth dropped open.

'What are you doing?! Stanley?'

Princy sank into a heap on the ground, clutching his ribs.

'You hurt him.' Miren's voice had gone all quiet and breathy, like someone had stolen all the air from her chest. 'That's not nice, Stanley!'

Princy clawed his way towards the window, shaking. Like an injured animal trying to get away from a lion.

Stanley grabbed for his ankle, but Miren stopped him cold. 'Leave him alone, you big bully!' Her voice was icy and desperate, like Princy being hurt was the worst thing in the world.

Miren scrambled off the bed and pounded Stanley's chest. Stanley had to work fast to catch the tank so she wouldn't pull the tubes out of her nose. She pounded and pounded, her tiny fists so weak it was like they were made of paper. After a few seconds, she ran out of energy and her hands drooped by her sides. She gathered up Princy's broken bones, tears oozing down her cheeks.

'Stay still, Princy. I'll put them back on. You go away.' She turned and glared at Stanley. He'd never seen that look on her face before, like she didn't even recognize him.

Princy sat up, eyes fixed on the ceiling. Miren tried to fit the ribs back into place, but they kept falling off.

'Look what you've done.' The tears dribbled into Miren's mouth, making her choke. 'You have to make them stay.'

'You don't understand,' he said, crouching down

next to her. 'Princy is bad. He's the one making you sick.'

Miren swallowed her tears and blinked up at him. 'No, Stanley. Is that what you think?' She wiped her face with the hem of her dress. 'He's my friend. My best friend. He makes me feel better, not sick.'

Princy did always make Miren laugh, but that didn't change what Jaxon had read in that book.

'I heard you talking to him the other night.' He smoothed down her crinkly hair, but she shrugged away from him. 'Didn't I? What did he say to you?'

'He told me that if I feel bad, I have to think of something funny. Like a duck with floppy feet or a pig doing cartwheels. Then I won't hurt so much.'

'That's all he said?'

'Yes, that's all he said.' Miren's eyes pleaded with him. 'You have to help me put him back together, Stanley. You have to.'

Thoughts whizzed around Stanley's brain like angry wasps, their stick legs pricking the inside of his skull. He didn't know what to think any more, but he knew one thing. He couldn't stand the way Miren was looking at him. Like he was a monster instead of her big brother. He never wanted her to look at him that way again.

'Fine, but you have to promise me something.' He turned to face Princy. 'You have to promise never to hurt my little sister. Not ever. Understand?'

Princy nodded. Stanley looked into his black eye sockets. Somehow they didn't look as deep or scary as before. Not at all like the picture in Jaxon's stupid book.

'You heard him, he promises,' Miren said. 'He's going to be a good skeleton.'

'Why doesn't he tell me himself?'

'He did, dummy. Didn't you hear?'

Stanley didn't hear anything. Princy buried his head in his hands, like he was crying, too.

'Help him, Stanley. Please – he said he'd be good.'

Stanley let out a deep-down sigh. 'All right, hold on, let me get some glue.'

Stanley dragged his dad's toolbox out from under his bed and fished around for some superglue. He found one tube that had dried up long ago, and another that had never been opened. He took that one with him and used it to glue Princy's three broken ribs back in place. The skeleton winced each time Stanley touched him.

'There you go, Mir-Bear. All better.'

Miren hugged Stanley's chest.

'I want to see Princy spin the ball some more.'

'OK, but just for a little while.'

Princy stood up and balanced the ball on the tip of his finger. He spun and spun, so fast the colours all blurred and became one moving rainbow. Princy seemed a little shaky at first, but after a while he started to bob his head and jiggle his toes. Tinkling music floated up from the floorboards. The tune was sad and happy at the same time. Soon, Princy started spinning right along with the ball.

He spun so fast Stanley couldn't see his bones any more, just a whizzing tornado of colour and motion and sound.

CHAPTER TWENTY-SIX

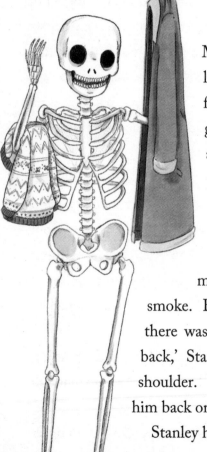

Mom came home a little later. At the sound of the front door opening, Princy gave the ball one final spin and then disappeared in a puff of pink smoke.

Miren stood on her bed and clapped. Stanley blinked, to see if Princy might be hiding behind the smoke. But even after it cleared, there was no sign of him. 'He'll be back,' Stanley said, patting Miren's shoulder. Whether Stanley wanted him back or not.

Stanley helped Miren into the living room. Her bare feet slapped the tiles, and she bounced up and down when she walked.

'Put it down,' she said. 'I can push the tank by myself.'

Miren greeted Mom at the door. 'Hey, baby. How are you feeling?'

In answer, Miren wheeled around and got tangled in her tubes.

'What's got into her?' Mom said. She sounded like she hadn't slept in weeks, and her jawbones stuck out more than ever.

'What happened, Mom?'

'Nothing, it's just been a long day.'

She took off her jacket and hung it on the coat stand next to Ms Francine's sweater. Only the coat stand wasn't there any more. In its place stood Princy. Mom dropped the jacket on to his outstretched fingers without taking so much as a second glance in his direction.

Miren saw Princy, too. She pointed and giggled so hard she started to wheeze.

'What is up with you today?' Mom said. 'Stanley, help me get her into bed. I think she's had enough excitement for one morning.'

'You sure everything's OK?' Stanley said. Mom never came home from work this early, after only a few hours.

'I'm sure.' She tugged at her frayed Walgreens vest. 'Can you put your sister to bed? I need to get these clothes off. And I need to make some calls.'

'Yeah, Mom. I got it.'

Ms Francine helped Stanley talk Miren into taking a nap. They read her a story, with Ms Francine doing the wolf voice and Stanley playing the pigs. Ms Francine did an amazing wolf. Then Stanley turned on Miren's favourite night-light, the one that made the walls look like rolling waves.

'Goodnight, Mir-Bear.'

'Sleep tight, little one.'

Stanley went into the kitchen and chopped cucumbers for Ms Francine's rusalka salad. He didn't believe Mom when she said everything was OK, but he didn't know what else to do about it. He wondered if Dad was one of the people she was calling, but he decided not to ask. Asking wouldn't make him call back any faster.

'Do you know this word, "rusalka"?' Ms Francine said. She stirred the pot of borscht, the steam curling her bushy eyebrows.

'No, does it mean cucumber?'

Ms Francine laughed. 'Most people think the rusalka

is a mermaid, but they're wrong.' She stopped stirring and tapped the side of her nose. 'The rusalka is a spirit that haunts a river or a stream. Maybe a pond, who knows? She waits for young men to pass by, and then she lures them into the water.'

'Why?'

'What do I know?' She swatted her hands at Stanley. 'I'm not a ghost. If you find one, go and ask her.'

Now Stanley laughed. As he chopped more cucumbers, he peered through the window that looked into the living room, and past that to the entryway. Princy was gone, replaced by the regular wooden coat stand.

'Do you think Princy's a ghost?' Stanley whispered.

'Princy? Who is this Princy? What a funny name for a skeleton.'

'Shh! Don't talk so loud.'

'What? No one is listening.' She smoothed her eyebrows back into straight lines. 'The skeleton is not a ghost. This I know. He is more like . . .' She thought about it for a long time, stirring the bubbling soup. 'Like an angel.'

Mom padded into the kitchen, wearing sweats and flip-flops.

'Can I help with anything?' She rubbed the

black bags under her eyes.

'You go rest. Stanley and I will finish up the borscht and put a batch of borsok in the oven. Won't we?'

Stanley shrugged.

'So modest. For such a little boy, he's a big help. You raise a good son with this one, Momma. Now go, get out of here, you lie down and we'll let you know when borsok is ready. And tea?'

'Tea would be nice.' Mom tugged her hands through her hair. 'I don't know what I'll do without you, Ms Francine.'

'You haven't got rid of me yet.'

Mom tried to smile. 'I think I'll go lie down. Wake me up if you need me.'

Stanley rolled dough into balls and even managed to eat a few spoonfuls of Ms Francine's special hazelnut filling when she wasn't looking.

'Good thing I don't have eyes in the back of my head,' Ms Francine said as Stanley gulped his third scoop of filling. She was facing the stove, so there was no way she could have seen him.

'Yeah, good thing,' Stanley choked.

Ms Francine made tea, and Stanley went to wake up Miren. He didn't find Princy anywhere in her room, but he did hear something moving around in the air vent that sounded suspiciously like clinking bones.

Stanley shivered. He didn't know if Princy was an angel or what, but that skeleton sure knew how to give someone the heebie-jeebies.

Thirty minutes later, Mom, Stanley, Miren and Ms Francine sat around the dining table eating crispy borsok and blowing on their tea.

'Miren has a doctor's appointment at three. Do you want to come with us, Stanley?'

'Yeah, I can help with her tank,' he said. 'Is that why you came home from work so early?'

Miren coughed into her cup. Mom patted her shoulder and held back her hair, but the coughing lasted a long time. When she finally stopped, Miren looked thin and pale, like the coughing had zapped all of her energy.

'You OK, sweetheart?' Mom said. She kissed Miren's ear and nose and forehead.

Miren scrunched up her mouth and moaned. Stanley had never heard her make that sound before. She grasped her chest, and silent tears dribbled down her cheeks.

'What's wrong, baby? Is it your chest?' Mom pulled Miren on to her lap. Miren sucked in a sharp breath, like it hurt when Mom touched her. 'Oh god, I'm so sorry.

Ms Francine, can you call Dr Cynthia? Her number's on the fridge, ask if we can come early.'

'Yes, don't worry, I call.'

Miren cried into Mom's sweatshirt. Stanley went to her bedroom and got her glow wand and some of her other toys. Nothing cheered her up. He even tried to juggle rubber balls, like he'd seen Princy do, but they just bounced on the table and splattered Mom's tea.

'Stop it, Stanley! Can't you just sit still and stop causing trouble?' Mom started to breathe fast, like Miren. 'I'm sorry, look, please go to Miren's room and pack her a bag. One set of clothes, a blanket, and some of her toys. Can you do that?'

'Do you think she's going to have to stay in the hospital again?'

'I don't know. Just do it, Stanley.'

Stanley packed the bag. When he came back into the dining room, Miren was laughing. Stanley couldn't tell why at first, but then he looked out the window and saw Princy doing cartwheels in the garden.

Miren gazed over Mom's shoulder, clapping and chanting, 'Go, Princy, go!'

Mom turned around and shook her head. 'Who is Princy? What are you laughing at?' She tickled Miren's tummy, and Miren doubled over in giggles.

Princy did the Running Man and the Robot and a bunch of other dance moves Stanley didn't know the names for.

'It's OK to go in early,' said Ms Francine. 'What should I tell this Dr Cynthia?'

Miren bounced in Mom's lap, the tears forgotten.

'Maybe we'll just go in at three, like we'd planned. What do you think, baby? Do you feel better now?'

'I feel better, Mom. Can we go play outside?'

They all went into the garden. Stanley danced around, trying to mimic some of Princy's moves, while Mom held Miren in her lap. No matter how much Princy swayed and waved and jiggled, Mom never once looked in his direction.

Like, to her, he didn't even exist.

Later, at the doctor's office, Stanley watched Mom's bag while she took Miren into the back to meet with

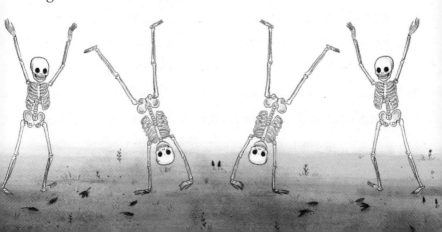

Dr Cynthia. Her phone kept buzzing.

Some of the messages were from Aunt Joan, Mom's sister. 'You know we're always here for you,' and, 'If you need help, just let us know.'

The phone rang again. The caller ID said Morris. Stanley flipped open the phone.

'Hello?'

'Oh, kiddo, it's you. Hey, I heard about your mom's job. Real bummer. Do you think I could talk to her for a sec?'

'What about her job?'

Silence on the other end. Uncle Morris sighed. 'Here I go again. Foot in mouth syndrome. Oh well, might as well tell you. Your mom lost her job, buddy. But no worries, OK? Uncle Morris to the rescue. I know it'll take some getting used to, but how would you feel about moving to Florida?'

'Moving to what?' Water crept up the back of Stanley's throat, like he'd swallowed an entire ocean.

'Florida, dumb-dumb. Land of a thousand beaches. Sun and surf and all that. Look, is your mom there?'

'She's busy.' Inside, he choked and gagged and flailed just to stay afloat, but outside his skin had gone numb.

Stanley hung up the phone and switched it to silent.

CHAPTER TWENTY-SEVEN

Stanley had just slipped Mom's phone back into her bag when Dr Cynthia came out of her office and walked straight up to him. He'd always liked how Dr Cynthia's hair twisted into dreadlocks on top of her head, but not today. She had a weird expression on her face, the way people look when they're pretending to be happy.

'Hello, Stanley. Sorry you've been waiting out here this whole time.' She placed a hand on his knee, but he pulled away. 'Why don't you come into my office so we can talk.'

She held open the door and waited. Stanley didn't move. He'd seen enough TV shows to know what would happen next.

'Take your time,' said Dr Cynthia, her fake smile faltering. 'Your mom and I will be waiting for you when you're ready.'

He watched Dr Cynthia leave. Why didn't Mom come out and get him herself? He settled into his chair, not planning to go anywhere, but another thought occurred to him. If he didn't go, Mom would have to listen to the bad news alone.

Mom could do a lot of things on her own, but he didn't want her to have to do that.

Stanley stepped into Dr Cynthia's office. It smelt like flowers, and a dumb stuffed hippo sat on the shelf behind the desk.

'Say hello to Dr Hip,' Dr Cynthia said. 'He keeps the place running when I'm gone.' Stanley didn't laugh or say hello, and neither did Mom.

Instead, Mom took his hand and guided him into the seat next to her.

'This won't take long. Dr Cynthia just wants to explain some more about Miren's condition,' Mom said through tight lips.

Stanley squeezed her hand while Dr Cynthia told them about fluid and lung function and something called valves. He didn't understand most of what she was saying.

She was still in the middle of talking when Stanley burst out, 'Hey, where's Miren? Why isn't she here?'

Mom's fingernails dug into his palm.

'She's going to stay with us tonight, in a room just on the other side of this building.' Dr Cynthia told him all about the room and the nurses who were going to keep Miren safe. 'You can help, too, Stanley.' She looked right in Stanley's eyes, but he blinked and looked away. 'She's going to be in a lot of pain.'

He stopped breathing, like someone had plugged up the back of his throat. Mom gripped his hand so hard it hurt. 'What can I do to help?' he said.

'Just be with her. Sit by her side, read to her. You'll know what to do.' Dr Cynthia found Stanley's eyes again. 'Stanley, your sister's condition is very serious. I need you to start thinking . . .' She took a deep breath and started again. 'You should know that your sister doesn't have much time.'

'That's enough,' Mom said in an ice-cold voice. 'He doesn't need to hear this.' She shot out of her chair and yanked Stanley's hand. 'Come on, let's go.'

'It's never easy to hear, but things are progressing quickly, Ms Stanwright. The sooner you accept what's happening, the better equipped you'll be to say goodbye when the time comes.'

'Shut up!' Mom spun around and then froze. Her eyes

opened wide, like she was shocked at her own words. She dropped Stanley's hand and rushed out of the office.

Stanley wanted to go with her – he wanted to run and run and never stop running – but instead he turned back. Even though it hurt just to open his mouth, he had to ask Dr Cynthia about Princy. He had to know if something like that could really make someone sick, but the words that tumbled out of his mouth like rotten teeth were, 'How long does she have?'

Dr Cynthia considered her words. 'There's never any way to tell, exactly.' She rubbed her temple. 'If I had to guess, I'd say a few months. But it could be weeks.'

As they walked across the building to Miren's new room, Mom jammed her headphones into her ears, and Stanley heard the echo of a robotic voice explaining how to get tangles out of dog hair. He had so many questions, but there was no point in asking. Mom wouldn't be able to hear him, and besides, he was pretty sure he needed to throw up.

Miren was in a room with purple curtains and a scratched white floor. She seemed so small and fragile in the big bed, it hurt Stanley's eyes to look at her.

'We should call Dad,' Stanley said, reaching for

the phone on the bedside table.

Mom squeezed her hand over his. 'Not now.'

'You heard what Dr Cynthia said.'

She shook her head and her lips twitched, like she was trying and failing to make them smile. 'I don't want to worry him over nothing. Miren will be better soon, you watch. What we need is a second opinion.'

'But Mom, that's not what—'

'I bet you're hungry after waiting so long,' she said. 'I'm going downstairs to get some dinner. Do you want to come?'

'No thanks,' Stanley said. 'I'll stay here and keep an eye on Miren.'

She nodded and left without saying anything else. Stanley stood next to Miren's bed, not sure what to do. Dr Cynthia had told him how he could help, but it didn't seem like it was enough. There had to be more.

After a few minutes, he reached for the phone and dialled Dad's number.

'Hello, Stanwright residence,' said a voice on the other end.

'Dad, you answered, it's Miren, she's—'

'I'm not home right now, but leave a message after

the beep and I'll get back to you as soon as I can. Bye now.'

There was a beep, then a dull buzz. Stanley listened for a moment before he clicked the phone back into its holder.

So much for Dad coming to the rescue. Maybe he'd call back – he had caller ID – but for now, he and Mom and Miren would just have to get through this by themselves.

Stanley decided to try Dr Cynthia's advice. He sat next to Miren in bed and read her a story. The words came out scratchy at first, but they got easier the longer he read. As he reached the part about the skeleton army raiding the castle, a white hand slid around the edge of the purple curtains.

Princy peeked out, saw Stanley, and gasped. He slid back into his hiding place, his bones shaking so much the silky purple fabric trembled. He was nothing like the warrior skeletons in Stanley's book.

Miren blinked and tried to sit up in bed. She had another set of needles stuck in her right wrist. The skin there was red and raw.

'Mir-Bear, are you awake?'

Miren struggled to pull the breathing mask away

from her face. Stanley didn't know if he should help her or not, but he decided it would be OK to lift up the mask just long enough for her to say something.

'My chest hurts. Stanley . . . I'm scared.'

Stanley put the mask back in place and closed his book. No stupid story about skeletons was going to make Miren feel better.

But maybe . . . the real thing would.

He stood up and threw back the curtain. Princy huddled into a ball on the floor, covering his ribs with his hands.

'I'm not going to hit you,' Stanley said.

Miren moaned, and both Stanley and the skeleton turned around to look at her.

'I need your help. You have to make her feel better. You can do that, can't you?'

Princy got up slowly and nodded. He held out his hands like he was asking Stanley a question.

'I don't know, whatever you want to do. Dance?'

Princy raised up one finger. Who knew brainless skeletons could have ideas? He picked up a bedpan and twirled it on top of his head. Stanley helped Miren sit up and slid his arm around her shoulders so she wouldn't fall out of bed.

They watched Princy balance the bedpan, a vase full of plastic flowers, and a metal serving tray on his head all at the same time. Miren moaned a little bit less when he tossed all three into the air and caught them one by one on the end of his big toe.

The objects balanced there for an impossible moment, and then Princy put them all back and disappeared into the bathroom just as Mom returned with dinner.

'Sweetheart, you woke up!' Mom pushed the tray of food into Stanley's hands and crushed Miren in a hug.

For the next hour or so they sat around watching TV and picking at their food. Finally, it was time for the news to come on, and Mom switched the TV off. She'd always said the news made her depressed.

Miren was getting sleepy again. She laid her head on the pillow and closed her eyes.

Mom put her plate on the rolling tray and scooted her chair closer to Stanley.

'We're going to get through this, just the three of us.'

'I know,' Stanley

said. Even as he did, five spindly white fingers poked out from underneath the bathroom door and waved at him. They would get through it all right, but he wasn't so sure it'd be just the three of them.

CHAPTER TWENTY-EIGHT

That night, Stanley slept in bed next to Miren, and Mom slept on a camp bed on the floor. Stanley woke up a few times to hear Mom crying. One of those times, he saw Princy sitting cross-legged beside her, stroking her hair.

She didn't cry any more after that.

Stanley had to go back to school the next morning. Someone from the head teacher's office had left Mom a message on her phone. He took a taxi to school.

He told Jaxon about Princy and the hospital after lunch. About how Princy wasn't really a monster like they'd thought, and about his talk with Dr Cynthia. He could see that Jaxon didn't really believe him about

Princy, even though he never said so.

'It sounds like cancer,' Jaxon said, dragging a fork through his macaroni. 'But you know how stubborn Miren is. If anybody can beat it, I bet she can.'

Stanley tried to think back to what Dr Cynthia had said. He remembered a lot of long, heavy words that made him sick to his stomach, but that was about all. If she'd talked about cancer, he'd made sure not to hear it.

'Maybe, I don't know. Look, let's talk about something else, OK?'

Jaxon nodded and dug around in his backpack for something. 'Well, I wasn't going to mention it, but there's a new message on the home page for the Young Discoverer's Prize.' He pulled out a brand-new iPad, complete with zombie-green cover, and handed it to Stanley. 'Read it.'

'Due to the high quality of entries submitted this year, the judges have decided to award two grand prizes. That's right. Two trips to go on expeditions with *National Geographic* to two mystery locations. Winners will be announced in a live broadcast on our website,' Stanley read aloud.

'They don't say the date, but you know what this means? You have twice the chance to win.'

'Yeah, I guess.'

Stanley should have been excited, but instead he handed the iPad back to Jaxon. With everything that had happened, the contest didn't seem important any more. True, he was desperate for Dad to come home, but winning some stupid contest wouldn't make it happen. Only Dad could decide to do that, and he and Mom and Miren were a good enough family all by themselves.

＊

When Mom picked him up from school, he could tell she'd been crying again. They went straight to the hospital and found Ms Francine waiting for them in Miren's room.

'Long time no see,' Ms Francine said. 'Here, I bought us cookies from downstairs. Not as good as tube cookies, but still pretty good.'

Mom left to go pick up some things from home. Stanley unwrapped his cookie and sat next to Miren's bed.

'She's been sleeping all day. Looking so peaceful, don't you think?'

'Not really,' Stanley said. He didn't know how anyone could be peaceful with needles sticking in their wrists and tubes up their nose.

'I'm so sorry about little sister, Stanley. You're a brave boy, you know that? It's never easy to lose someone you love.'

Stanley bit off a chunk of cookie. It tasted like cardboard and caught in his throat.

'Ms Francine, do you think the skeleton is the Grim Reaper?' The words spilt out of Stanley's mouth. He felt better once he'd said them, like a weight had been lifted from his shoulders. Even though he was pretty sure Princy was OK, he couldn't help still having doubts.

'Ah, the one with the hood and the big, curvy stick?'

'It's called a scythe,' Stanley said, feeling like Jaxon.

'Look at the old man who knows everything. But you want to ask Ms Francine if this skeleton that grew in your garden is bad or good, yes?'

'Yes.'

'What is bad and what is good? Some things, little Stanley, just happen. Flowers grow one day, and they blow away the next. The sun goes up and down. This skeleton, does he make your sister feel better?'

Stanley nodded.

'Then you have your answer. He is good.'

One of the machines behind the bed started beeping. Miren's skin had gone cold and grey. Nurses rushed in and wheeled her down the hall behind another set of swinging doors. Stanley tried to follow, but a nurse yelled at him to stay back. He stood on his tiptoes and watched doctors in white coats swarm Miren's bed. He couldn't see what they were doing.

'Come, Stanley, let's go back to the room and wait for Momma.'

Stanley didn't move. The doctors brought out more machines. They stood in a circle, blocking Miren from view.

After a while, Stanley's ankles grew tired and he couldn't watch any more. He thought about how scared Miren must be, and he wished Princy could go in with her and hold her hand, since Stanley couldn't.

He peeked through the window one last time, and he thought he saw a bony toe sticking out from underneath Miren's bed. It wiggled in his direction, then drew back into shadow.

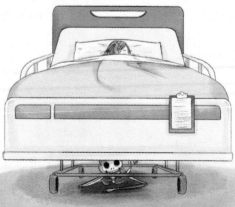

CHAPTER TWENTY-NINE

Miren stayed in the emergency room long after the sun went down. Mom paced the hallway when she got back and refused to eat anything. She wouldn't even drink a glass of water. Finally, one of the doctors in white coats came out and pulled Mom aside.

'Miren is a strong little girl, Ms Stanwright.' The doctor flipped through some pages on his clipboard.

'Just tell me if she's OK.' Mom dug her fingernails into her palm.

'She pulled through, but she's going to have to stay with us for a while. Dr Boyle can meet with you first

thing in the morning to lay out the treatment plan.' The doctor handed Mom a packet of papers from his clipboard. 'This is the insurance paperwork you need to fill out. One of the nurses can help you if you have any questions.'

Mom reached out to take the papers, and Stanley saw three bloody half-moons from where her nails had been.

———

Later that evening, Stanley and Ms Francine sat beside Miren's bed, back in the room with purple curtains. Mom started to fill out the insurance papers but stopped when she got halfway down the first form.

She slid them into the bin without saying anything. Stanley heard her in the hallway later arguing with a nurse.

'Are we going to have to leave?' Stanley asked Ms Francine. 'Since Mom lost her job?'

Ms Francine clucked her tongue. 'Nobody is going to leave. Why would we leave? Miren is sick, so the doctors help her.'

'Doesn't somebody have to pay?' Stanley said.

'Listen to you, sounding like a grown-up. Momma is worried and scared. She doesn't want Miren to be sick, so she thinks maybe if she doesn't sign the papers, everything will be OK again.'

'How do you know?' Stanley said. Ms Francine could always tell what everyone was thinking. He wished he could do that, even a little.

'I know.'

Mom did sign the papers, and Miren stayed at the hospital. For that night, and the one after. Mom wanted Stanley to start sleeping at home, with Ms Francine watching over him, but he refused to go.

'I want to be with Miren. Especially, you know, if she's not going to be around for very long,' he told Mom, and she didn't say anything after that.

Miren spent the next few days sleeping, mostly. Stanley liked it when she was sleeping, because that meant she wasn't coughing or wheezing or crying into her pillow.

On Friday night, Ms Francine brought balloons and a board game called Hungry Hungry Hippos. The game was fast and loud, and Mom almost smiled once when her hippo swallowed five marbles in a single bite.

Princy peeked from behind the curtains just as Stanley

jumped out of his seat after winning his third game in a row. Stanley had suspected Princy was hiding back there for a while. The curtains looked lumpier than normal, and the windows kept making this weird jangling sound.

Ms Francine raised her eyebrows and nodded to an armchair by the cupboard when she saw him. 'Maybe he wants to play.'

'Who wants to play?' Mom said.

Stanley couldn't believe his ears. What was Ms Francine doing? Mom turned around and looked at the armchair, following Ms Francine's gaze. She stared at it for a long time, like she was trying hard to make sense of what she saw.

'Who are you talking about?'

'Oh, nobody.' Ms Francine swatted her hands. 'You know us old women, always talking to ourselves.'

Mom got up to check on Miren, and Ms Francine winked.

That night, Stanley woke up to find Princy sitting by Miren's bed, holding her hand. His eyes no longer looked scary at all, but kind of sad and peaceful. Like two dark oceans.

Jaxon and his mom came to visit on Saturday morning. The two moms went out into the hallway to talk. Jaxon stared at the tubes and the needles and the beeping machines. He picked at his thumbnail so long the tip broke off and he had to throw it in the bin.

'My grandpa died when I was seven, did I ever tell you that?' Jaxon said.

Stanley shook his head.

'Yeah, I was with him when it happened. We were sitting on the couch, watching cartoons, and then his head fell to one side. I remember, because it conked me on the shoulder, and I yelled, "Ouch!" and then I saw his face. He looked just like Grandad, except I knew somehow he wasn't any more. You know what I mean?'

'Miren's not going to die,' Stanley said.

Jaxon swallowed hard and went back to tugging on his fingernails.

CHAPTER THIRTY

Miren started her treatments on Monday. Stanley didn't understand why the medicine that was supposed to help made her cry more than ever. She threw up twice into the basin next to the bed.

Stanley cleaned Miren's face with a wet towel. He squeezed her hand and read her a book Ms Francine had brought from home: *Charlotte's Web* – one of Miren's favourites. Nothing he did could make her stop crying.

Then a pair of bony fingers popped up out of nowhere and tiptoed across Miren's blanket. Stanley had never even noticed Princy folded up under the bed. The fingers twirled like a ballerina up Miren's arm and on to her shoulder. She stopped crying. It was a miracle. She stared at the fingers. One flicked her cheek, and then the hand skittered away on to her tummy.

Miren laughed and laughed inside her breathing mask. Mom couldn't understand what she was laughing at.

'Probably just something from *Charlotte's Web*,' Stanley explained. 'Pigs are kind of funny.'

'I guess,' Mom said.

Princy slid his other hand on to the bed and made a bone butterfly that fluttered and swooped above Miren's head.

Mom lifted up Miren's mask so she could talk.

'Look, Momma. Can't you see it?' She pointed, and Mom's eyes searched the air, trying to see what Miren saw.

'What is it, sweetheart?'

'A butterfly, look at how its wings change colour!'

'You're so silly. Stanley, did you read her a story about a butterfly?'

'It's not a story, it's a butterfly.' Miren's forehead got scrunchy.

'If you say so.' Mom laughed. The sound made Stanley happy. 'I'm just glad you're feeling better. How about I go get you some ice cream?'

'Ice cream? All right!' Miren punched the air, just like her old self.

'That settles it, then. Three ice creams.'

———

That night, Miren had to go to the emergency room again. The doctor said the treatments made her too sick. When he came in and said that to Mom, Stanley got so mad he pretended he was punching Slurpy over and over in his head, until he turned to a stinky, green smear. How could the doctors be stupid enough to give Miren medicine that made her feel worse?

Princy stayed by Miren's side all the time after that.

None of the other grown-ups could see him, as far as Stanley could tell. Except for one nurse in poodle scrubs named Jamie. She always looked right at Princy when she came into the room. She frowned when she saw him but never said anything.

It started to rain again on Sunday. Mom went downstairs to call Dad, and it was about time. Stanley found out he'd been leaving her messages ever since Stanley had called from the hospital phone and hung up.

Ms Francine wasn't there, either. She'd gone to New York for a few days to visit her brother. He was in the hospital, too, because he'd been in a car accident.

Even Princy had disappeared. Stanley hadn't seen him since the day he came into Miren's room wearing a lab coat and a clown wig. Miren had laughed so hard Mom asked the doctor if she might be having some kind of weird reaction to the drugs.

With everybody gone, it was Stanley's job to take care of Miren. She was sleeping late, as usual, and so Stanley decided to take some of the money Mom had given him and go downstairs to buy doughnuts. Stanley knew they had the kind with sprinkles, Miren's favourite. That way, when he came back, she would wake up to a special treat.

He picked out three doughnuts and got in line to pay.

A hand reached out of nowhere and grabbed his elbow. Stanley twisted around to see Princy looming over him, a grave expression on his face. Where had he come from?

A little boy in front of Stanley pointed at Princy and screamed.

'What is wrong with you?' said the boy's dad. 'What did I tell you about inside voices?'

Princy squeezed Stanley's arm harder and tugged him towards the exit.

'I haven't paid yet,' Stanley whispered. He felt stupid talking to an invisible skeleton. Well, sort of invisible.

Princy kept pulling. Something in his eyes told Stanley he'd better follow. They took the lift back up to Miren's room. Princy's reflection in the shiny steel lift doors looked fuzzy, like something floating behind wet glass. If Stanley didn't know for a fact there was a skeleton standing beside him, he might not have even noticed him.

Princy led Stanley into Miren's room. The skeleton didn't follow, but instead stood blocking the exit, like a security guard. Stanley walked slowly up to Miren's bed. Her eyes flickered open when she heard him.

'Stanley.'

'Mir-Bear.'

'I'm tired, Stanley. Did you get my doughnut?'

'How did you know I was going to get you a doughnut?'

Miren shrugged. She lifted up her hand, like she was reaching out to take her doughnut, but Stanley didn't have one to give her. He'd left the bag in the cafeteria. Miren's hand collapsed back down by her side.

'Maybe you should rest now, Mir-Bear. You look sleepy.'

Miren blinked and scrunched up her forehead. 'Bye-bye, Stanley. I'll miss you.'

'Don't you mean goodnight?' Stanley said.

Miren closed her eyes. Her hand felt cold in his.

'Mir-Bear?' he said, and that was when the machines started to screech.

CHAPTER THIRTY-ONE

White coats surged through the doorway and pushed Stanley aside. He wanted to tell them that it was too late, that Miren was gone, but they had already wheeled her into the hallway towards the emergency room.

Stanley watched the doctors take Miren away. He touched his face with numb fingers. The swinging doors banged open and shut. The lights overhead turned grey, like someone was slowly dimming the bulbs. Stanley might have stood there in the hallway forever if he hadn't seen a white shape disappear through a door off to his left.

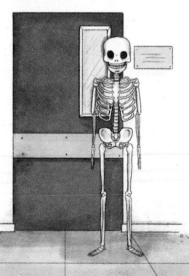

Stanley ran after Princy, punching open the door to the stairwell. Footsteps click-clacked in front of him. Stanley hurled himself forward, taking the stairs three at a time.

'Get back here – !'

He wanted to yell at Princy, call him the worst names he could think of, but Stanley's throat had turned to ash.

He pounded down floor after floor until he finally reached the bottom. A door slammed in front of him. He shoved it open and came out into an underground parking garage.

He didn't see Princy at first, but then he heard the tap-tap of his bones hitting the ground. He saw Princy running up the ramp leading to the street.

Stanley raced after him. His thighs burned and needles poked into his lungs, but he didn't care. Princy reached the pavement and slipped into a crowd of people. Stanley had to find him. He crashed into a man carrying a newspaper, knocking the coffee out of his hands. The man yelled at him, but Stanley couldn't hear. White noise rushed between his ears, like an avalanche.

He caught sight of Princy, first behind a news-stand, and then over by the bus stop. People cursed and screamed as Stanley shoved his way through the crowd. He almost caught what he thought was Princy on the other side of the bus stop, but it was only a poster advertising DentalFrost toothpaste. A big white dollop sitting on a bristly white brush.

Stanley scanned the crowd. A breeze caught his face, and he realized that his cheeks were wet. Had he been crying?

He looked across the street, and that was when he saw Princy slide into a dark alley. He ran after him.

'Stanley, stop!'

Mom caught him in her arms and pulled him out of the intersection just as a taxi screamed to a halt. The taxi driver honked and peeled away.

'What were you thinking? Why aren't you inside?

God, Stanley, you could have been killed.'

Mom dug her nails into Stanley's arms.

'What's wrong?' Stanley didn't answer. 'Stanley, talk to me, is everything OK? Why are you out here?'

Stanley knew his mom would only get angrier if he didn't say something, but he couldn't make the words come out. He shook his head, and then he crumpled on to the pavement.

'Stanley, tell me what happened!' Mom was yelling, but Stanley could barely hear her.

Tears filled his nostrils and choked the air from his lungs.

'Is it Miren?' Mom said, her voice like glass. 'Is she OK?'

Stanley shook his head, and then Mom was the one who started to cry.

CHAPTER THIRTY-TWO

They held Miren's funeral on a Thursday. It had rained the night before, but that morning the sun came out and made the leftover raindrops sparkle. Stanley didn't remember much about the funeral, except that he kept looking around for Princy, but he was gone.

Dad didn't make it back for the service, either, but he sent Stanley an email.

'Stan the Man, I'm so sorry about what happened. I wish I could be there for you and Mom, but my flight just got cancelled. They can't get any more flights out until tomorrow. Trust me, if there was any possible way I could make it there I would. You guys are the most important people in the world to me. I hope you know that. Love, Dad.'

Stanley wanted to be angry, but he wasn't. After what had happened, being angry didn't seem that important.

Mom said she was too sick to attend the funeral, but she insisted that everyone go on without her. Ms Francine said it was because she couldn't accept the fact that Miren had died.

'These things take time,' Ms Francine said, burying Stanley in her fuzzy sweater.

She came to stay at the house after the funeral. Dad kept saying he would come, too, but there was always a case or a meeting he couldn't miss.

'Some people love with their whole heart, like you and Momma,' said Ms Francine one afternoon over a pot of steaming borscht. 'When bad things happen, it hits them right in the centre of their chest.' She pressed a bony finger into Stanley's rib cage. 'Other people, like this papa of yours, keep love tied to the end of a long stick. That way, even if their heart gets broken, they never feel it inside, in the place where it hurts.'

'He doesn't even care,' Stanley said.

'The heart has a way of coming back home, whether we like it or not. Some day, this papa will blink and find his heart sitting back inside his chest, where it always belonged. That day, he will care about the hurt he caused you.'

'Today, it's up to us?'

'Good thing Ms Francine cares more than a hundred papas.'

And it was up to them, Stanley and Ms Francine, to take care of Mom the best way they knew how. She hadn't eaten or come out of her room since that last day at the hospital.

'Love is like that, too,' said Ms Francine, 'but don't you worry, little Stanley. One day, Momma will wake up and see.'

'See what?' Stanley said.

But Ms Francine just winked and went back to stirring the borscht.

———

Ms Francine ended up staying for two whole weeks. During that time, Stanley would go sit with Mom on her bed sometimes, but she never once came out into the living room or talked to anyone.

At some point – he couldn't remember when – he started sleeping outside in the tent. The house was too stuffy and too full of Miren's things.

Stanley was out there one night, lying on a blanket, looking up at the stars, when he heard soft footsteps disturbing the wet grass. His heart caught in his chest. He turned around, half expecting to see a skeleton creeping up behind him, but it was Mom.

She sat down on the blanket and put an arm around him. She didn't say anything. They sat like that for a long time, watching the stars. They must have fallen asleep, because some time later, Stanley woke to the sound of tinkling music.

He blinked, unable to process the scene before him. Miren leapt through the air, wearing a gown made of flowy white fabric that looked like clouds. She danced and spun and pirouetted, her hair glittering in the moonlight. And she wasn't alone.

Someone held her hand. Princy whizzed and pranced and flew alongside her. He was wearing a red velvet vest with puffy gold sleeves. Miren danced with him and smiled. Smiled so wide her whole face glowed.

'I see her,' Mom said.

Stanley looked over to find that Mom had woken up beside him. Her eyes followed Miren's and Princy's fluid, sweeping movements.

'Do you hear that?' Mom said, looking puzzled. 'It sounds like music.'

'It is,' Stanley said.

'I don't understand.' Mom scrunched up her forehead, just like Miren used to do. She looked deep into Stanley's eyes. 'She's really gone, isn't she? My little –'

She couldn't finish. The word caught in her throat. She buried her head in Stanley's shoulder and cried for the first time since that day standing in the street outside the hospital.

⊶——⊶

Mom started eating again after that. She came out of her room and washed her hair, and a few weeks later she found a job as an assistant manager at JoJo's Coffee Spot.

It was around that time that Stanley got a letter in the mail. He stood on the kerb and opened it, wondering who on earth could be writing to him.

'Dear Stanley, thank you for entering the Young Discoverer's Prize annual contest. Each year, we receive dozens of entries from all over the world. We regret to inform you that your entry was not selected as one of this year's winners . . .'

Stanley skipped down to the bottom of the page, where someone had added a handwritten note: 'Your image got great feedback! More likes than any other entry. Unfortunately, the picture was too blurry for any of the judges to make out. Better luck next time.'

For some reason, that made Stanley laugh. So hard he swallowed his cinnamon gum.

'What's wrong?' Mom said, waiting for him by the garage door.

'Oh, nothing.' Stanley crumpled up the letter and tossed it in the big green rubbish bin next to the house.

———

Later that week, Stanley helped Mom pack up all of Miren's things, except for Ashleigh and Stripy Pony and all of her pictures. They put those on the mantel over the fireplace. He went back to school after that. He'd missed a lot of work, but he made it up eventually. The rest of that year passed in a blur. They flew down to Florida for Thanksgiving, and before school started in January, Mom came into Stanley's room one night and asked him if he'd like to move to Florida.

He didn't want to at first. It felt kind of like leaving

Miren behind, but then he remembered how much Miren had loved the beach that one time they'd visited Uncle Morris for her birthday.

'I think she would like it there,' he said, and Mom hugged him and nodded like she knew just what he meant.

Jaxon came over a few days later to help Stanley pack. They put some stuff in boxes, but mostly they played *Skatepark Zombie Death Bash* and talked about everything but the fact that Stanley was leaving and they'd probably never see each other again.

'You know they're making a Darby Brothers' movie,' Jaxon was saying, 'and it's coming out on the last day of school, so we should definitely . . . oh.'

For a moment, Stanley had that feeling like when you rip off a plaster, only this time the plaster was covering his whole body and Ms Francine wasn't there to give him cookies from a tube to make the sting go away. 'We can still watch it, though, when it comes out online. I can call you, and you can tell me all the parts that don't match the books . . . except, my computer's a piece of junk . . .'

'I might have a solution for that.' Jaxon pulled a crumpled gift bag from his Darby Brothers' Just-in-Case investigator's backpack and handed it to Stanley. 'It's a going-away present.'

The thing inside looked thin, like a book or . . . 'An iPad?'

'The same one you found buried in your garden. I cleaned it up, though, and it still works like new. That way we can talk and stuff without waiting for your computer to load.'

Stanley woke the screen and a picture stared back at him. Jaxon, Stanley, and Miren posing in front of the ice-cream shack at Lazlo's Pizza and Mini-Golf. He gripped the iPad so hard his fingers went numb. The picture changed; now it showed Miren holding her gardening tools, bars of sunlight warming her face. In the background, Ms Francine and Uncle Morris hunched over a smoking grill. Jaxon had taken the photo the year before, at Miren's birthday.

More pictures flashed on the screen. Miren, Mom, and Dad at kindergarten graduation. That year Miren had dressed as a tomato for Halloween, and Stanley and Jaxon had gone as lumpy cucumbers. Stanley drew in a long breath and slid down so his head was resting on his beanbag chair. A gentle weight pressed on his chest and held him there.

'I can delete the pictures if you want,' Jaxon said, picking at his fingernails. 'They were Mom's idea anyway. Sorry, Stanley.'

'No.' Stanley forced the words through the sticky wall at the back of his throat. 'It's perfect.'

Ms Francine came in just as Jaxon was leaving. She was wearing the scarf Stanley had bought her as a kind of reverse going-away present, fuzzy wool with a goat eating grass stitched on one end.

'So this is goodbye,' she said as Jaxon and Stanley stood on the porch, staring at their feet. 'Why so sad? You will see each other again. Close or far, what does it matter? By now you should know, little Stanley, that the ones you hold dear never leave you.' She patted the locket hiding under her blouse. 'They travel with you wherever you go. You keep them here . . .' She tapped Stanley's chest. '. . . and here, in your head.'

'I guess so,' Stanley said, but her words made him feel lighter, like the pressure on his chest had lifted and he could breathe again.

A week later, Ms Francine helped them pack up all of their things in a big moving van, and Uncle Morris flew down so that he could do the driving. Jaxon stood on the kerb, waving goodbye, a real goodbye this time, and so did Ms Francine. Stanley hated to admit it, but he was going to miss her stories about goats and her woolly sweater and maybe even her borscht. On the way to Florida, they sang songs and played car games, and Uncle Morris told so many fart jokes Stanley said he should probably get a world record.

On the second night, they stopped at a Happy Trails petrol station to stretch their legs. Stanley and Uncle Morris sat on the bonnet of the van, staring up at the purple-streaked sky. Mom went inside to buy snacks, and when she came out she said, 'Here you go, little Stanley.' She handed him a cup full of steamy liquid. 'Eat your cocoa before it gets cold.'

Mom and Stanley laughed, while Uncle Morris shook his head and looked at them like they were crazy. The whole thing would have made Stanley sad if Mom hadn't already told him Ms Francine was planning on visiting the next summer, and making them borscht every night. Whether they liked it or not.

It took three days to get to Uncle Morris's house. It was three times the size of their old one, and only a few yards away from a big, sandy beach.

'Go ahead, kiddo, check out the water.'

Stanley flung off his flip-flops and ran across the sand. The beach stretched so far on either side he couldn't see the end of it. The ocean crashed in front of him and made him think of Miren's night-light, the one that looked like rolling waves. He splashed in, just enough to get his feet wet. The water was warm, even though it was the middle of winter.

He dug his toes into the cool sand, and his big toe hit something hard.

A lump filled his throat. He fished around for the hard thing and pulled it out of the water.

It was small and white and about the size of a finger bone. He wiped the wet sand from the sides, his stomach dropping.

When the sand came away, he saw that it wasn't part of a finger, but instead a shell. The kind that's hollow inside and swirled to look like a unicorn's horn. A blast of cold wind slapped Stanley's face. He let it wash over him, and then he turned around and called back towards the house.

'Come on, Mom, Uncle Morris, let's go swimming! Last one in's a rotten nobody!'

Stanley dunked his head under the water. He opened

his eyes just for a second, and even though the salt burned, he imagined he saw Miren down there waving at him.

Just Miren.

And she was smiling.

ACKNOWLEDGEMENTS

My agent, Brianne Johnson, is a fearless advocate who brings a little magic to everything she touches. I am so lucky to be working with her and the entire team at Writers House.

One of the best days in my life was the day I received an email from my editor, Mallory Kass, expressing her passion for this book. No one will ever be able to match her love, enthusiasm, and dedication. I am so grateful to Mallory and everyone at Scholastic who have worked tirelessly to bring this story to life.

To all of my writer friends who have helped me along this journey, I would have been lost without your fellowship and encouragement.

Finally, to my misfit, soul-sister puppy, Hera. Although you may not be able to read this, you bring light wherever you go, and I thank you for your kind soul and constant companionship.

ABOUT THE AUTHOR

Kim Ventrella is a children's librarian and a lover of weird, whimsical stories of all kinds. She lives in Oklahoma City. *Skeleton Tree* is her debut novel.

ABOUT THE ILLUSTRATOR

Victoria Assanelli was born in Buenos Aires and spent most of her childhood playing with her grandparents, reading books and drawing doodles. She was a textile designer before becoming an illustrator. She loves drawing fairies, princesses and all things whimsy and dreamlike.